W9-ATW-836

OTHER BOOKS BY LILA HOPKINS

Young Adult Fiction

Talking Turkey
Eating Crow

Nonfiction

Victors In The Land

WEAVE ME A SONG

For Dollie + Earl,
Whose lives weave a song
of love!
Psalms 121: 1

WEAVE ME A SONG

by

Lila Hopkins

A novel: A chronicle of family devotion,
a story of love, betrayal, forgiveness and reunion.

High Country Publishers, Ltd

Boone, North Carolina
2002

Copyright (c) 2002 by Lila Hopkins

All rights reserved under International and Pan American Copyright Conventions. Published in the United States by:
High Country Publishers, Ltd.
197 New Market Center #135
Boone, NC 28607
(828) 964-0590
Fax: (828) 262-1973
www.highcountrypublishers.com

Library of Congress Cataloging-in-Publication Data

Hopkins, Lila.
Weave me a song : a novel : a chronicle of family devotion, a story of love, betrayal, forgiveness and reunion / by Lila Hopkins. – 1st ed.
    p. cm.
ISBN 0-9713045-7-2 (hardcover : alk. paper)
1. Appalachian Region, Southern—Fiction. 2. Grandparent and child—Fiction. 3. North Carolina—Fiction. 4. Women weavers—Fiction. 5. Grandmothers—Fiction. 6. Art dealers—Fiction. 7. Sick—Fiction.
I. Title.
PS3558.O063546 W43 2002
813'.54—dc21

2002003331

Manufactured in the United States of America
First edition: October 2002

Acknowledgments

I am grateful to the fine weavers at Crossnore Weaving Room who demonstrated tirelessly, answering many questions. I had access to the fabulous private library at the Weaving Room. Thank you.

Ellie Hjemmet of Roan Mountain, Tennessee, a master weaver, critiqued and corrected the first draft. Thank you, Ellie.

This book could not have been written without a special group of friends – the High Country Writers. Maggie Bishop critiqued the first draft. Jean Shoemaker and Marian Coe provided vital suggestions on Chapter One. Joyce Blanton proofread my final draft; Ann Beardsley proofread the typeset copy.

Among those others in HCW who encouraged me, I must mention: Dottie Isbell, Judy Geary, Bill Kaiser, Carolyn Houser, Barbara Ingalls, Jane Wilson and Alyce Nadeau. Your e-mails and calls kept me going.

Judy Geary, and Barbara and Bob Ingalls make dreams come true. The artistry of designers Schuyler Kaufman and Russell Kaufman-Pace make them more beautiful. I am forever indebted to them.

Thanks to each of you!

Lila Hopkins
2002

DEDICATION:

For Richard:

my gentle man of faith

WEAVE ME A SONG

by

Lila Hopkins

Chapter One

S*he was bruised,* alone and frightened out of her wits, but she was going home. What else could matter? Unless she was too late.

The Greyhound bus followed the interstate from Charlotte, its diesel engine rattling. Freddie Gouge leaned against the window to watch smoky exhaust being swallowed by gunmetal gray clouds.

She ignored the pain in her gut. The hunger gnawed her insides like a carnivorous weasel, nibbling away at her confidence and self-esteem. No food would tame her hunger, that she knew well.

The bus seat was larger than her seat on the plane; however, a catnap was just as elusive on the bus. Leaning back and closing her eyes, Freddie tried to sort out her emotions. The single most important element in her life was Gram; her worst inexplicable blunder was leaving Gram and Pax.

She had hoped it would not rain on her homecoming, but the somber overcast of clouds over western North Carolina contrasted dramatically with this morning's dazzling sunlight at Sky Harbor International Airport in Phoenix. She squinted at the skyline, straining to see the first faint traces of the mountains. When she could make out a pewter hump on the horizon, her heart lurched. The Blue Ridge Mountains. Paxton Palmer.

Mountains and Pax. She drew a painful breath from deep within her lungs. He had been courteous on the phone, but he had been speaking on behalf of Gram. Freddie touched her hair. It had the texture of dried straw and was bleached dry by the sun. Her skin was several shades tanner than the girl who had left the state soon after high school. She hoped, at least, for a chance to wash her face before confronting him.

The whine of the bus's laboring engine, shifting down for its final climb to Morganton, alerted her that her journey was nearing its end. Exhaustion and anxiety wove a tight knot in her chest. It was hard to imagine her feisty little grandmother seriously ill.

She could be home within an hour, if someone met her. Home. She had been away so long that the word had an unfamiliar ring to it. What would she do if Pax hadn't arranged a ride for her? Hitchhike the forty-seven miles? She felt just desperate enough to try it.

As they pulled into the station yard, she watched the surge of people moving toward the bus. She scrutinized each face, searching for a former neighbor or friend who could give her a ride on the final portion of her journey.

Her travel plans had been so rushed and confusing, flying on standby, she could not give Pax the itinerary. She had changed planes three times, spending hours waiting in airports and bus stations. She left him a message on his answering machine during a layover in Nashville, but had no way of knowing if he had received it.

The clouds had dissipated; at least it wouldn't rain. Searching the crowd, she saw him, looming above the heads of the others. Her heart dropped to the pit of her stomach. Why couldn't he have sent someone else to meet her?

He looked detached, isolated, but she saw nothing menacing in his stance. He was slightly away from the group, and with his broad shoulders and height, he looked like John Wayne meeting the stagecoach in a Western movie. She had forgotten how masculine he was. His full brown beard distinguished him from all the other men in the crowd.

She gathered her belongings but deliberately waited until the aisle was filled with other passengers. She stood up stiffly, weak with foreboding and wishing she could postpone this encounter. How would he welcome her?

As the driver helped her down the steps, Pax spotted her, and stepped forward. His face flooded with relief, as though he had not really expected her.

"Hey," he said and reached for her suitcase.

"Hello, Pax."

"This it? This all you've brought back?" He sounded incredulous. "Then you don't intend to stay." He chopped his words off.

"If . . ." she began, but he did not look at her.

He grunted and took her elbow. She was startled by the force of his grip as he propelled her toward the parking lot. "Ouch!"

"Sorry. Didn't mean to hurt you."

"It's okay, Pax. Have you been waiting long?"

"About four years, more or less." He took a deep breath, released her arm and looked down at her. "No, I haven't been here long. Over here. You remember 'The Green Bullet'?"

Freddie patted the fender of his ancient truck. "I can't believe you still drive this thing. Where's your stepladder?" She had forgotten how high the cab was.

He placed her suitcase in the truck bed and opened the door of the cab. "You haven't grown much in the years you've been away." He grasped both elbows and lifted her as easily as he had in high school.

She leaned against the seat and waited for him to get in. Her insides churned. She had prayed that seeing him would not reignite old feelings.

She focused on the bluish haze of the mountains in the late afternoon. Soon she would be able to smell the trees – pine, spruce and fir. Only forty-seven miles from home and Gram! Less than an hour.

Pax ducked under the door frame, and she was acutely aware of him as he climbed in beside her. Before he turned the ignition key, she laid her hand on his arm. She felt his muscles stiffen at the contact, and it sent a shiver through her body, but she did not remove her hand immediately.

"How is she? Truthfully?"

"Fred, I've always told you the truth. She's been mighty sick, but she rallied when she heard you were coming. You'll be shocked when you see her, I guess – although she's come a long way. She's up part of the time, but she walks with a cane." He cleared his throat. "Didn't think her worn-out ticker could make it, but you know what a stubborn old girl she is."

A cane? Freddie had not realized Gram was that frail. "Why didn't you call me sooner?"

"Couldn't find you."

"Gram knew how to reach me."

"Your Gram was unconscious." He sounded defensive. "I did the best I could." His eyes slid over her hair and face. "You look about dead. Close your eyes and rest a bit."

She squirmed uncomfortably under his appraisal. He lifted a trembling hand, cupped it to fit the contour of her cheek. For a heart-thumping moment she anticipated a caress to her face. She met his eyes, and he dropped his hand back onto his knee. Sadness rolled over her. Why had she expected him to touch her? Why did she want it so much?

She lowered her eyes, and he jerked his gaze back to the dashboard and fumbled with the keys.

She tried to squeeze the fatigue from her voice. "Close my eyes? And miss something? Not on your life. Are the leaves turning? What about the mountain ash? Are the berries red yet?"

He chuckled unexpectedly and started the engine. "They're getting there! I spotted a sentinel maple coming down here. The ash berries are still kind of orange, though."

It was an easier homecoming than she deserved, and she was encouraged as some of the weariness drained away. She exclaimed over each new view of the mountains. He seemed pleased, and he pulled off the road to an overlook to give her a better sight of Grandfather Mountain.

"I've missed it so much."

"Then why in thunder didn't you come back?" The question stung her, and tension hung in the cab between them.

"I'm not sure I can answer that," she said quietly. How could she explain to Pax what she didn't understand herself? Her throat felt dry and prickly. She watched him maneuver the truck back onto the highway, his eyes straight ahead, his jaw muscles taut.

"I wasn't planning to interrogate." He glanced at her, then gave his attention to the road. Some emotion she could not identify passed over his face. Anger? Contempt? Sorrow?

"It's not that I won't answer – I just don't know how. Oh, Pax," she said. "I'm so sorry."

He put his hand on hers. "It's okay, kid. I've adjusted." He spoke gently.

"And you've found someone else." It was a statement, not a question. The wistful tremor in her voice embarrassed her.

He dropped his shoulders in a noncommittal shrug and she felt closed off from him. The loneliness that had stalked her for months rose in her chest and seemed to close the flow of air in her throat. She stared out the window.

Suddenly everything began to fold in on her. She wanted to lean against him, hide her face in his shoulder, beg for forgiveness! All the years away from him! She could hardly stand to sit so close to him without touching him, but she had severed her rights to him four years ago. She did not see a wedding ring, yet she dared assume nothing.

He remained silent, and an uncomfortable solitude filled the cab as she listened to the rumble of the engine when he down-shifted on the climb up the mountain.

####

Pax slowed before the last curve and long ascent to Grandmother Garnet's house. There was enough light to make out the large "GG" on her mailbox. It was her trademark in the weaving industry. Gram was the "Grandma Moses" of Appalachian weaving.

Freddie's trepidation increased when they rounded the curve, and she could see that most of the house was dark. She had somehow expected to see the diminutive figure of her grandmother waiting for her on the porch of the aging house.

The gray house blended into the smoky gray mountains and the darkening gray sky. She could scarcely make out the outline of the roof. Something was missing. "Where's Dollie?"

Pax seemed to anticipate her question. "I'm sorry, Fred. GG didn't tell you that your dog died three years ago? I hope she warned you that the big oak tree went down in the blizzard last year."

"No," she whispered. "She didn't." In the last remnants of the fading light, the house looked naked without the protection of the huge oak she had loved all her life.

"We planted a sugar maple, but it'll take years to make a difference. GG refused to take another dog."

"She must be in bed."

"Probably. Don't worry, she'll welcome you with open arms. You act like you expect the hickory stick. Wail until I come around to help you."

She wanted to leap out of the truck and race up the steps into the house, but a fear of what she might encounter restrained her. She was grateful for Pax's strong arms as he lifted her down and steadied her. She noticed how quickly he stepped back from her as soon as they reached the porch. Did he have to be so obvious in his rejection of her?

The walk across the porch was the longest she had ever taken. How would her grandmother look? She hesitated, and Pax finally reached around her and opened the door. He flipped the light switch and the familiar old porch was illuminated. She turned, thirsty for the familar sight. Beyond the railings, an evening fog was just rising, an undulating wisp of white, but beyond that, nothing.

The house smelled musty, and Freddie shivered. She could see the lights in the hallway, spilling out from her grandmother's room.

"Gram," she called. She wanted to run to her grandmother as she had as a kid but her legs wouldn't cooperate. She dragged herself toward the doorway, then paused, unable to enter.

Propped in the huge bed was a small figure, pain-pinched face ashen against the white pillows. She reminded Freddie of a doll she'd had as a child. The face had been made from a genuine apple, shriveled and wrinkled by the sun. Now Freddie desperately searched the wizened face for any sign of welcome.

"Gram?"

Freddie saw her grandmother's eyelids flutter and then widen as she saw her. For an incredibly long time, Gram studied her, saying nothing, focusing on the closely-cropped, too-blonde hair and the sad, tortured face.

Freddie reached up to fluff her hair and tugged at the hem of her wrinkled blouse. Everything blurred as she read the only response she had ever seen in her grandmother's face: absolute, uncompromising love – whether she deserved it or not.

"Well!" the old woman said in a stern voice. She wet her parched lips and her tone lost its gruffness as she held open her arms and whispered, "Come home, child."

"Oh, Gram!" Freddie sprinted across the room to her grandmother's waiting arms. She sank onto the floor beside the bed and buried her head in the quilts.

"Hush, child. You're home now. Everything's all right. Isn't everything all right now, Pax?" The knotted, blue-veined hands gripped Freddie's with surprising strength.

"Yes, ma'am," Pax replied and his voice was husky. "I'll get her suitcase."

Gram released Freddie's hands and stroked her hair.

With Gram's caress, all the pain of the past four years came to the surface.

"Don't cry, child. We don't have time for that. Stand up and let me see you."

It took effort but, as unsteady as a newborn colt, Freddie struggled to her feet. She moved back to concentrate on her grandmother.

"Child, you look like a lost creature in the darkest woods. Plum feverish."

From the doorway, Pax asked, "Where's Marge?"

"Sent her home. Didn't want no one but family for the homecoming."

"I'd better . . . "

"No, you ain't," the old woman said testily. "You ain't leaving until you eat some of the apple pie Marge fixed. I've waited all evening for my piece. Freddie, you remember Marge Burleson, Harry's widow? She's been helping me a while." She waved a bony hand. "You know where the kitchen is."

It was all too much. Freddie still felt guilty for not having been home when Gram needed her, but at the same time her heart was racing, singing of Gram's acceptance, Gram's loving welcome. She was home at last.

"Paxton Palmer." She could hear Gram's chiding voice from the bedroom. She had come alive. "Tell me why it took you so long to fetch her. I figured forty-five minutes each way. Figured you'd be back 'fore dark or I'd of left the lights on." Her voice rose with crackling good humor. "You stop along the way to sweet-talk a little?"

Paxton sounded appalled, and a bit angry. "GG, you know better than that!"

Freddie's neck and face burned, but she felt reassured. Her grandmother felt well enough to tease and to order them around.

"Actually," Pax replied, "we stopped to look at the mountains."

"Ha!" Gram snorted in disgust. "Should of remembered I was waiting here alone."

Pax spoke quietly. "Sorry, GG."

Beside the pie on the table was a tray loaded with pottery mugs. Coffee this late for Gram? Seeing the sugar bowl and creamer, she knew better than to protest. She prepared the coffee, glad for the diversion that gave her time to collect herself.

# # # #

Later, when she carried the dishes back to the kitchen, Freddie reflected about the evening. She marveled at the apparent normalcy of the conversation. They talked about her plane trip and there were a few impersonal questions about the West and the desert, but nothing was mentioned about why she had left or how long she had been away.

The only sadness of the evening was Freddie's realization of how quickly and completely her grandmother wore out. When she returned from the kitchen, Gram was asleep and Pax was gone. She hadn't thanked him for meeting her bus.

All at once, she felt the full impact of the day. Though exhausted, she was unable to go to bed, and quietly closed Gram's bedroom door. After pausing outside the bedroom, listening to the regular breathing, she wandered through the little house, dreading to go upstairs alone to her room. She wished Pax had not left so quickly.

In the living room, she found her grandmother's table-sized weaving loom. It had been draped with a white sheet as a dust cover, giving concrete evidence that her grandmother had not worked in some time. Freddie carefully lifted the sheet and shook off the dust, sneezing as she did. She stroked the maple wood on the beam. Would GG ever weave again?

She turned on another light and studied Gram's work. At first she was delighted with the flow of the design and the subtle colors that seemed to blend like a fall breeze fluttering autumn leaves. Then she felt trepidation. Something was wrong. Something was very wrong.

She carefully unhooked the latches and examined the roll on the take-up beam. The first part of the weaving was perfect, but the rest looked as though the artist had lost her way. Freddie touched the yarn and lifted the shuttle to examine the weft. According to the swatch, it should contain a soft gray. Instead, the bobbin that fit into the shuttle was wound with a flaming scarlet yarn.

It was as though a different weaver had taken over. This was totally unlike her Gram's work. Was her grandmother losing her mind? Freddie felt sick to her stomach.

Long before Freddie had appeared on the scene, Gram had made a name for herself when she was still raising her own sheep, spinning and dyeing her own yarn. She hadn't been GG then; that came after she was a grandmother and began winning state and regional awards. Her signature of Gouge had slowly evolved to Grandmother Garnet and finally reduced to GG.

The lights seemed to dim, time blurred and a small girl sat beside the fireplace, listening to the rhythmic thump of the beater as her grandmother operated the loom.

Occasionally Gram sang a few bars of a favorite hymn:

"When the roll is called up yonder, I'll be there."

Most of the time she just hummed the hymns and concentrated on her draft, taped to the top of the loom. The work was physically draining and she conserved her energy.

The thumping was hypnotic, and the child grew sleepy. The steady beat of the loom provided her a lullaby, and she felt safe, secure in the ordered pattern of her life.

Every once in a while, she would go stand behind her grandmother and dream of the day when she could manage the big loom. Gram said they had both cut their teeth on a hardwood boat shuttle.

Perhaps it was simply the scent of the wool

her grandmother and great-grandmother had spun and dyed, but Freddie was sure she could identify her Gram's work in any gallery. She used to boast that she could walk through blindfolded and locate her wall hangings.

Even after the spinning wheel had been replaced by a stack of colorful yarn catalogues, Gram had always given meticulous attention to detail and craftsmanship. Her distinctive combinations of color and exquisite patterns had put her art in a class by itself. This weaving looked as though the weaver had gone berserk. Gram was in worse shape than Freddie had realized.

She replaced the protective sheet. The loom stood like a silent apparition, guarding a somber secret, and the ghostly composition seemed to overcrowd the room oppressively.

She must talk to Pax about this, but Pax was off limits to her now. The first rift in their relationship came when they quarreled over the loss of Gram's original designs. She had spent months collecting them, only to have them disappear from Pax's office. Freddie's anger had lingered because Pax was too busy to hunt for the designs, he said. Setting up his gallery took all his time, and she had felt left out and lonely.

Gram never made an issue about his losing the designs and he was probably still her agent and adviser, but he'd made it abundantly clear that Freddie had no claim on him now. A terrible sense of isolation accompanied her up the stairs. She didn't care if she made him uncomfortable, she decided, she was going to see him tomorrow.

She was too tired to worry about it now. She only knew she was grateful that he had found her in

Carefree. Carefree. The name was an antithesis of what she'd felt in that town!

What a mess she had made of her life! Yet, as she undressed, she remembered the love and forgiveness in her grandmother's eyes. The one constant of her entire life had been Gram's unconditional love. Always.

What if she were to lose Gram? The unthinkable thought kept her awake for hours. She'd already lost Pax.

Chapter Two

Lying in the dark, Freddie remembered a scene she had not thought about in years. She had been busy with her weaving when she became aware that Pax was in the hall doorway, staring at her.

"Why are you watching me, and how did you get in here?" She caught the maple shuttle with her left hand and froze at the loom.

Pax didn't budge. Left shoulder jammed against the doorframe, arms folded across his chest, legs crossed at the ankles, he formed a diagonal exclamation mark in the doorway.

"You *are* cute to watch, but I'm *not* trespassing. Your grandmother invited me in." He uncrossed his feet, shoved away from the doorframe and walked into the room. "I didn't mean to interrupt. I love watching your look of absolute concentration. You wrinkle your brow like it's the most absorbing thing in the world."

"It *is* a difficult pattern," she mumbled, suddenly self-conscious. She reached up to brush the back of her hand across her forehead.

"But you're a master craftsman. Someday I'll own a gallery and feature your work."

####

Paxton Palmer was not local as they said in the high country. He transferred to Ash Hill High from Philadelphia his sophomore year. His father taught Latin and his mother was an artist. He was an outsider, but his interest and respect for her artistry won Gram over.

He began dating Freddie his senior year. On his first date with her, he discovered GG's loom. Coming up the front steps, he heard the thumping of her beater. Intrigued, he framed his face with his hands and peered through the door window.

Freddie jerked open the front door. He hurried past her to go in and stare at the loom. "What's she doing?"

She probably thought he was an idiot, but he didn't care. Something grabbed his attention and he could not let go. "Once the cat's out of the bag," his mother said often, "he'll chase it until he catches it."

"I know she's weaving, but what's the process?" He looked at the beam and dropped to one knee to study the pedals.

The dignified old woman sat erect at the loom as though she presided at the console of a cathedral pipe organ. "Young man, I ain't deaf. You might address me." She continued working.

"Excuse me, ma'am. I didn't want to interrupt your work. What do the pedals do?"

"Wal, they change the sequence of the pattern." She shoved the beater back, and showed him the weft and warp threads, and explained the difference. "See, this here's my draft. Tells me which pedal to punch."

"Like a big computer," he said.

"Huh?"

"Ingenuity and creativity aren't peculiar to high tech. You're doing what the computer does, only it does it faster. I'm impressed."

The ball game had to wait as Gram warmed to her favorite subject and explained the specific functions of her loom. Pax studied the moving parts and followed the process for each procedure she demonstrated.

"Do you spin your yarn?"

"Nope. Used to."

He grinned. "If this isn't the coolest thing!"

Gram looked perplexed, then said, "Yep. It's up to scratch. And it appears you got your wool neatly wound into butterflies."

"I don't know what that means," he said.

Freddie explained it deliberately, slowly as though to a child. "When you're doing some kinds of weavings, like tapestries, you can wind your yarn into small fingerwound skeins called butterflies."

Freddie finally managed to pull him away, shaking her head.

He stammered, "Mrs. Gouge, I hope I didn't offend you." He bowed to her.

"It's a compliment. And a compliment, boy, that I was paying you, explaining it all to you." She gave a robust guffaw.

Moments later, in the car, he said, "I didn't mean to be rude. I was interested."

Freddie laughed. "I've heard of girls competing with beautiful sisters, but I hadn't expected to compete with Gram and her loom."

"Sorry about that. Do you know the wood carver, Storm Bartholomew? He can coax a face out of a piece of wood like you wouldn't believe."

"Are you an artist?" Freddie asked.

"No. My mom is. She does still lifes. I've visited loads of galleries with her and my dad. It's sort of a hobby with us. I'm going to enjoy getting to know your granny – and you. She's almost as much fun as you are." Pax grinned wickedly.

"Why are you so interested?" She sounded skeptical.

"I'm curious about everything. I like art, but the process of creating really fascinates me."

"But you're not an artist?"

"No. I'm intrigued by the creator and by the creation."

"To exploit?"

"Exploit? Why would you think that?"

"I don't think that. But Gram got tricked out of most of her weavings by a dealer who sold them for thousands of dollars." She bristled with anger.

"I'd never exploit an artist. God, don't ever let me do that."

The last was not directed at her but she continued to slip furtive glances at him all the way to the gymnasium.

The year he graduated, Pax's parents returned to Pennsylvania. He enrolled at Appalachian State University and worked in an art gallery in Boone. When his grandmother left him a small legacy, he bought an old building on the river near Linville, remodeled it himself and opened his own gallery.

"I've always had an eye for beauty," he told Freddie. "That's why I wanted a gallery and why I love to hang out with you."

Even so, building his gallery and stocking it demanded long days and nights. Their dates became less frequent.

####

Freddie whispered to the black walls of her bedroom. "I'll never have anything hanging in your place, Paxton Palmer." She wondered about his gallery and how much it had changed. She knew that tomorrow, no matter how difficult it would be, she had to visit it to talk with him about Gram's work.

Chapter Three

Freddie wrestled the vintage Ford into the parking lot at the Palmer Gallery and paused to get her bearings. The building looked different, grander. Impressive. Pax had enlarged the gallery and remodeled the entrance. Gram hadn't mentioned that. Pax must have found a windfall. A flicker of suspicion drifted across her mind. Surely Pax had not profited from the "lost" designs without sharing with Gram?

She forced the thoughts from her mind; no time for recriminations now. She needed what he might know about Gram's condition.

It had not occurred to her to dress up for this visit but now she felt out of place in her faded blue jeans and knit shirt. She sat with the window of the ancient Ford rolled down, toying with the steering wheel, hoping the song of the river would calm her before she went in to face him.

Pax, hunting the prettiest location he could find, had selected the site by the river. When he took her to see it, he said, "People who can paint or sculpture or weave, do. Those of us who can't master the crafts sell them. I want a place worthy of the beautiful objects I expect to sell." Apparently he was successful, judging from his recent renovations.

An electronic bell softly announced her arrival, and her heart quickened. She had wanted to go in unobtrusively to look around before seeing Pax. As she entered, her eyes widened appreciatively. From the outside she thought he had made the gallery too sophisticated, and that it might not be suitable for the location. Inside, she was delighted with the decor. The showroom lacked the polished glossiness of the big city galleries with lots of glass and lights. There was an earthy, homespun atmosphere about the place. A huge tree trunk dominated the room, presenting a mountain ambience. A low stone wall curved around it, providing a welcome bench for visitors. The limbs of the tree were used to display intricately carved birds and colorful pottery birdhouses.

Freddie's gaze followed the branches up, leading her eyes to a loft containing a series of paintings of the mountains. The blues and greens of the Blue Ridge scenes glowed under a huge skylight. At the landing on the stairs, she recognized a wall hanging that could have been created only by her grandmother. Its placement gave it a prominence above everything else in the gallery. She drank in the beauty.

Throughout the showroom, Pax had placed single item tables that showed off exquisite pottery highlighted by tiny penlights. The wide-planked pine floors were unlike the expensive carpet of the galleries in Phoenix, more direct, somehow, as if Pax felt no need to mask the commercial aspects of the business. Another interesting display caught her attention – a sitting area featuring handcrafted children's furniture and toys. It was different from anything she had seen in any other gallery. She started toward it.

Until now, she had seen no one, but a well-modulated voice stopped her.

"Good morning. Are you looking for anything specific?"

Freddie turned to face a tall, raven-haired woman, moving with elegance toward her. Thin heels created a staccato accompaniment on the polished floor.

"Welcome to the gallery."

Freddie stammered. "N-not really. I-I wanted to see the gallery and to talk with Pax."

"Freddie!" Another woman's voice pulled her gaze up to the loft. "I heard you were back." A young woman emerged from a doorway under the eaves, pulling packing crates with her.

"Hello, Susan." Freddie responded to the former classmate and childhood friend. "I didn't expect to see you here."

"Did you meet Elaine?" Susan bumped down the staircase, carrying an armload of packaging material, dragging boxes, and babbling on with a nervous energy Freddie remembered well. "Elaine Saunders – Pax's right hand man. Or, I should say, woman. Elaine, meet Frederica Gouge, GG's granddaughter."

Elaine gave her a frank appraisal and laughed. "Frederica Gouge. Grandmother Garnet. No wonder you chose Freddie and she goes by GG. Excuse me. I didn't mean to be rude. I love GG's work. I adore GG."

"So do I." Freddie wanted to be indignant, but she was disarmed by the friendliness in Elaine's manner.

"So what do you think of the new showroom?" Elaine said.

Susan interjected, "Isn't it about the grandest thing on the mountain?"

"It is, indeed. I didn't know. I mean, I was so surprised. When did Pax build it?"

"After Elaine became his partner."

"About two years ago," Elaine explained. "Have you seen Pax?"

"Sure, she saw him. He met her at the bus station last night."

Elaine maintained her poise. "This morning? Have you seen him this morning? He's back in the shop." Elaine seemed to simply project rather than shout. "Pax!"

Pax pushed the door open. His eyebrows shot up when he saw Freddie. "So, what do you think? Is it 'cityfied' enough for you?"

"It's marvelous, Pax. I've had enough city to last a lifetime. It has a wonderful mountain charm."

A grin stretched across his face. "Elaine and Susan run the place, but the charm is all mine." Pride gave a lilt to his words. "Come on back. I'm building a new showcase. " He was wearing work clothes, and sawdust stuck to the hairs on his arms. He held the door open, and she slipped under his elbow into his shop.

She felt a surge of warmth as he moved around her. She had forgotten how tall he was and for a moment was overwhelmed by the sheer size of the man. He exuded a confidence and contentment that made him glow, she thought, if it were possible for a giant of a mountain man to "glow."

The shop was totally unlike the showroom. It was small and crowded, and smelled of sawdust, stale coffee and the acrid scent of lacquer. The only part of the gallery that seemed familiar to her, it was located behind the office area. Freddie remembered that Pax was far more at home in his shop or office, dealing with hopeful artisans, than in the showroom, catering to critical customers. Elaine seemed far more suited to that angle of the business.

"Let me wipe off a box for you to sit on." Then, without looking at her, he said, "What's up?"

"What do you mean?" She felt uneasy, wondering if he resented the interruption.

"I mean, something brought you in here early your first day. Is something wrong?"

"I'm not sure." She eased herself slowly down on the pine box. "I wanted to thank you for meeting me in Morganton. You got away before I remembered my manners last night." She took a deep breath. "Have you seen Gram's new weaving – the one she's working on now?"

"No; you know she never lets me see her work until it's finished. Is something wrong with it?"

"Yes. Drastic blunders." She shook her head in disbelief.

He had picked up a plane and returned to his project, but at that he laid the tool down and turned to look at her. "I don't understand. Her work gets better and better. She understandably hasn't finished anything recently."

Freddie dusted off her shirt. She did not want to meet his eyes. "Would you come to the house and take a look at it? I don't trust my judgment."

"I'm not sure she'd let me see it."

"Come after she's gone to bed. Unless you have a date."

"Elaine usually closes up, anyway. Any pie left? I'll be there. About eight?"

# # # #

Freddie stopped briefly at the grocery store and then sped home, reluctant to spend time away from her grandmother her first morning back.

Driving up the narrow driveway, she sighed. The elegance of Pax's establishment contrasted sharply with the signs of neglect at Gram's place. At one time she thought she had secured a decent financial future for her grandmother, when she gathered all the original designs that her grandmother and great-grandmother had produced. She swallowed, and her throat felt raw.

Marge had settled her grandmother on the front porch where the sun splashed late summer warmth across her lap. She had a spectacular view of the mountains, but she had rarely spent time on the front porch during the morning hours. Freddie remembered a bundle of boundless energy, busy at work in her house or garden when she was not at her loom.

Today she was frail looking, wearing a heavy sweater and with a blue afghan draped across her legs. Her cane hung over the back of her chair.

Freddie set her plastic grocery bags on the floor and dragged another rocking chair up beside Gram. "I miss Dollie."

"Yes. Must be a sad homecoming."

"Sad? No! Oh, Gram, everything is beautiful and green."

"Must seem so after the desert."

They sat quietly until Freddie ventured, "I stopped by Pax's gallery."

Gram chuckled and pulled her shoulders straighter. "Land's sake. Didn't waste any time."

"What do you mean? I wanted to thank him for meeting my bus."

"I didn't mean nothing. Just tickled you wanted to see him's all." She rocked energetically.

"Gram, please. Don't try to stir anything up. There can be nothing between Pax and me again. Anyway, he's found someone else."

"Oh?" The old woman slumped back down into the chair.

"You hadn't told me he enlarged the gallery."

"We haven't talked about much of anything yet," Gram said.

No, Freddie thought, they hadn't. So much explaining. Where would she start? She sighed. "What do you want to know, Gram?"

"Nothing." She spoke so quietly that Freddie had to lean toward her to hear. "Everything. But I'm too tired now. Hand me my cane and help me back to my bed. Can't twist around to get the dad-burn cane. What matters is that you're home again. I just don't know why you left."

"I don't know if you'll ever understand. You never left the mountains."

"Yes, I did. Once." She smiled. "And that's when my Del – "

"You left Ash Hill? When?" Freddie was intrigued. "Tell me about it, Gram."

"Later, child." She shuffled toward the door. "It was a long, long time ago."

Chapter Four

Garnet Holloway was deter-
mined to work. In the mid-nineteen twenties, Avery
County was one of the poorer sections of the Appalachian region, and women did not have many vo-
cational choices.

When Garnet saw an ad in the bimonthly
county paper for a nurserymaid just across the state
line in Tennessee, she asked her brother, who had
traveled to Memphis, if there were mountains
around Johnson City.

"Small ones that you might learn to tolerate,"
he said.

Del Gouge, the only boy she had ever dated,
drove her to the bus depot in Elk Park. He was tall
and lanky and had a voice as quiet as a mourning
dove. He made it clear what he thought. "You're
too scrawny to be a nurserymaid, and you're still
wet behind the ears. Ain't knee-high to a grasshopper. They won't hire you, so you are wasting your
time and mine."

Garnet stiffened her back. "I'm seventeen. Old enough to know what I want to do."

"Clothes wouldn't wad a shotgun, and you can't hardly reach the gas pedals to drive. How could you be a nurse?"

She rose to her tiptoes, cuffed him on the chin and climbed onto the bus.

The dirt road wound through deep canyons and climbed a high pass, but when the terrain grew less rugged and the taller mountains drew back, Garnet's heart began to tighten. Each mile away from Ash Hill saddened her more. When they crossed the Tennessee line and stopped in Elizabethton, she caught the next bus back to North Carolina.

Del was sitting patiently on the bench in front of the General Merchandise and Seed Emporium.

"How'd you know to wait for me?" she asked.

"Oh, I knowed all right, and hoped. How far'd you get?"

She answered as though she was training for a journey around the world. "Twenty-eight miles."

"Better'n me. Time I left, I got off in Roan Mountain and hitchhiked back to God's country."

When she read about a crafts co-op in Atlanta a few months later, she talked about taking some of her weaving to Georgia.

Del said, "Ain't no reason to."

"Don't you have no faith in my work?" She nearly shouted at him, hands at her waist.

"Got enough faith in your work," he said quietly, "to know you can do anything here you could do in Atlanta. Plus, I'd hate to come all the way down there to fetch you home."

She stared at him, lower jaw slack. "Land's sake, why would you have to come fetch me back?"

He kicked the front tire on his Model T truck, whipped a handkerchief out of his back pocket, and wiped his brow. "Shoot, Garnet! I'll build you a room large enough for your loom and we'll fill the house with young'uns so you won't have to be no one else's nurse."

"Is this some kind of a proposal?"

"I reckon it's about the only kind you'll git from me."

And so they were married. They would have forty-nine happy years together, seasoned with depression times and the trials of eking out a living. The hard times drew them closer together. He built her a room for her loom, but they were not so successful with the children. Their only daughter, Lenore, died in infancy. They waited ten years before they were blessed with a son.

They named him Clyde after Del's brother who had died in the war.

A restless boy, Clyde left home at sixteen for a job in construction in Charlotte. He brought home a wife, but she didn't take to mountain living and they returned to the city.

Garnet found solace in weaving, often demonstrating at the Sloop School in Crossnore, and winning a whole collection of blue ribbons at county and state fairs. When she had no money for yarn, she made rugs, using worn-out clothing cut into ribbon-sized widths and twisted into thin strips.

Del's first Christmas gift to her after Lenore's death was a pair of sheep. She learned to shear them, bought a spinning wheel and a huge copper dyeing kettle. She whiled away hours of loneliness at the loom, trying not to dream of more babies. She'd never expected to be barren.

On her sixty-fifth birthday, Clyde returned home to live, bringing a small daughter clutching a worn cotton doll. "Her mother doesn't want her. Ran away – again. Will you help me take care of her? He presented Garnet with the tiniest, most forlorn-looking two-year-old Garnet had ever seen.

"Here's your granddaughter," Clyde said. "Kiddo, this is my mama."

Garnet knelt before her and smoothed golden hair back from the fragile face. She kissed a smudge on the top of the little nose.

"Mama?"

"Gram," Garnet said.

The child's upper lip quivered. She studied Garnet with wide, solemn eyes. Finally, she let go of her father's hand and raised hers, hesitated, then stroked her grandmother's mouth and chin with a tiny finger. She yielded to a gentle embrace.

Del sighed. "She's just a little bit of a thing."

"Ain't as tall as the door handle and weighs less than a bag of chicken feed," said Garnet and a surge of near-worship flooded her heart.

Clyde's eyes were brimming with tears when he confessed, "I didn't know what else to do, Mama, but to bring her to you."

"You did right, son," Del said. "She's in good hands. Both of them are, 'cause I reckon they need each other."

Later, after she had bathed her, washed her hair and put her granddaughter to bed, Garnet told her son, "I ain't calling her no silly name like Frederica."

"Call her Fred," Clyde said.

"Humph! Fred is a name for a big old man and she's only a mite of a child. She's Freddie to me."

Del called her "Little Bit," and he adored her.

"Wait until you see her mad," Clyde said. "Stiffens, throws herself on the floor in a tantrum. Picking her up's like trying to handle a greased eel."

Her grandfather said, "I'm glad she's scrappy! Pathetic little thing. I'd be mad, too, if my mama ran out on me. She has a little spark of Gouge in her. Makes me right proud." He laughed.

That night Garnet, sitting in her flannel robe, stared into her mirror for a long time. Her eyes were faded, a washed-out blue. She inspected the gray hair and studied the sags under her chin. She rubbed her wrinkled cheeks, remembering the caress of a tiny finger.

"You can handle it, girl of mine." Del stood behind her, his hands on her shoulders. "God ain't gonna give you nothing you can't handle."

"He'd best spoon up heaps of wisdom, and energy, then."

"He will, Garnet. I reckon He will. You'll raise a fine one. Yer eyes are already shining with love."

"I ain't worried about loving. Loving's easy."

Family life became rich and full for each of them, but it was a challenge for Garnet. She despaired over managing Freddie's hair. The color of corn silk, it was as fine as the spun glass "angel hair" she used on her Christmas tree.

"Drat!" she said. "I can spin cotton or wool, but this is like taming goose down." She finally learned to plait two long pigtails and later, to style a neat French braid.

She sewed by hand, tiny, delicate stitches, making dresses pretty enough for a princess.

Freddie followed her around like an affectionate puppy. She pulled up a stool to watch Garnet cook and padded after her from room to room. Her grandpa made a broom for her and she imitated her gram, sweeping the worn pine planks with an energetic swing.

As immaculate and careful about her housework as her weaving, Garnet delighted in finding a willing pupil. She taught the child to make a bed, and Freddie could snap the sheets like her gram to make them lie smooth, and she learned to make precise, tight folds at each corner of the bed.

In the spring Clyde broke ground and they planted a garden together: English peas as soon as the ground thawed, and beans on Good Friday. Gram insisted on a row of flowers in the middle of the garden: zinnias, marigolds and purple cosmos.

"I plant them 'cause they're pretty." She knelt between freshly plowed rows of sweet-smelling soil and Freddie knelt beside her. "Also, I heard on the radio that marigolds kill nematodes."

"No! Don't!" Freddie's eyes widened with horror.

Garnet squinted at her. "Hey? Don't what?"

"Kill them toads! I like them toads."

Garnet laughed so hard she toppled off her knees and sat in the dirt. She took off her sunbonnet and fanned her face as the tears ran down her cheeks.

Freddie was hurt and puzzled. She wanted to run back to the house to hide.

"Child of mine," her grandmother said, "you're the love of my life. God give you to me to make life plumb worth living. Land's sake, child, I ain't killing no toads. Nematodes are root-destroying insects."

Freddie smiled, climbed to her feet and curtsied to her grandmother.

They cultivated squash, onions, cabbage, potatoes, turnips, corn, and herbs for doctoring.

"I can remember when we used to tote our corn to the mill to get it ground into cornmeal," Garnet said. She told her about barn raisings, bean pickings, quilting parties and all the old mountain customs as they weeded in the garden.

"You afraid of snakes?" Freddie asked when she was three, going on four.

"Ain't many snakes here – too high up. Saw one in the hen house once, though."

"Grandpa kill it?"

Gram gave her a rare, withering look. "Killed it myself. Chopped its head off. Ain't afraid of a dumb old snake. But," she added, "I ain't got a thing for a snake to do, neither."

Del died when Freddie was six. She cherished the toys he had whittled. Her prized possessions were the rocking chair, her broom, and the loom he had made her.

It never bothered Garnet that she was past retirement age; nor did she care that she was older than the mothers of Freddie's classmates. Her grand-daughter was bright and loving and happy. Garnet figured she was doing something right.

The child seldom spoke of her mother, but once Garnet heard her asking her father about her. "When I'm grown, will I run away too?"

"You do and I'll skin you alive," he replied.

But after Clyde died in a construction accident on a dam site near Johnson City, Garnet lay awake worrying on lonely winter nights. Could an old mountain woman give a young girl all the training and advice she needed to get along in the world? She listened to the wind howling around the little cabin, marooned in an ocean of snow with only the deer and fox for company, and she wondered if she could adequately prepare her granddaughter for life outside their little hollow.

She made sure Freddie kept up her homework and got to school and Sunday school on time, but she couldn't afford music lessons or entertainment, so she did the only thing she knew to do. She taught her to weave. She had no choice.

Chapter Five

One afternoon when Gram left her work unattended briefly, four-year-old Freddie eased herself up to the loom. She hoisted herself up onto the bench and with a small hand pressed flat on either side of her, shifted her body and settled into the warm spot where her grandmother had sat. Her legs dangled high above the pedals.

Undaunted, she leaned forward to grab the shuttle, nearly toppling off the bench. Her grandfather had made several favorite shuttles for Gram, fashioning them with a drawing knife and cutting the holes with an auger and coping saw. This one was made from close-grained hardwood, sanded smooth as marble. Freddie ran her finger over the yarn on the loaded bobbin inside the shuttle.

She knew that the function of the shuttle was to carry thread across the warp, but she couldn't understand exactly how to accomplish the task. She managed a good-sized tangle before Gram rescued her weaving.

"Now, what are you figuring on doing next?"

Freddie, mortified, looked down at her hands. Her lips puckered and then she brightened. "Sing a song, maybe?"

So, the lessons began. Del built a small loom for his granddaughter and placed it beside Gram's, crowding other furniture out of the small living room. Gram was a patient teacher and Freddie an enthusiastic student. Sometimes the weavers sang together – an unlikely duet with Gram's quavering voice and Freddie's high one.

"Amazing grace, how sweet the sound,
That saved a wretch like me!"

Freddie stumbled over the words and for years sang about being a "witch."

Tonight, as she prepared for Pax's visit, she remembered the experience and she chuckled.

####

When Freddie's dad bought their first small black-and-white television set, Garnet scoffed about the "dad-gum newfangled contraption" that demanded *both* eyes and ears. It distracted from her weaving. She never learned to enjoy television. Her contempt for it continued into her eighties, but she had an addiction to nighttime radio. Freddie leaned against the bedroom door and listened to the monotone voice of a talk show host and relaxed a little, reassured that Gram had gone to sleep.

After filling the coffee pot and warming the pie, she returned to the living room to wait for Pax. She brushed her fingers through her short hair. The Arizona sunshine had been harsh on it. She was glad, however, that she had chosen a pink blouse because it complemented the mahogany color of her eyes.

Sitting alone in the semi-darkness, watching for his truck lights, was *deja vu* for Freddie. She wrapped her arms around herself and thought dejectedly of the evenings in the past when she had anticipated his arrival.

Who would have dreamed that a lost file folder would become the first wedge between them? Perhaps without that first rift, Brad would not have had a chance.

Brad.

She shivered. What possessed her to give up solid, dependable Pax for a dashing playboy? Her girlfriend in Arizona told her she was naive, but he had been so much fun, and contrasted sharply with Pax. Life was a big party to Brad and she had been captivated by his suave manners and promises, baiting her with a pledge to feature her as "artist in residence" at his gallery in Scottsdale. It hadn't taken her a week to realize what a fraud he was. She confronted him and unleashed a violence that ended the relationship.

She remembered the evening she had waited for Pax, to tell him she was breaking their engagement and going to Brad in Phoenix. It tore her apart to remember the pain and hurt in his eyes, but he gave up so easily she wondered how much he really cared.

Always before, his arrival had been announced by the joyful welcoming bark of Dollie, but the woods were quiet tonight. Finally, she saw a beam of light down the mountain and watched it flicker back and forth across the valley, sweeping tree tops as his truck swung up the twisting road.

She heard the whine of the old engine and wondered how he could afford a gallery renovation on such a grand scale.

She turned on the outside lights and stepped to the porch to greet him. The floor vibrated as he came up the stairs. As big as he was, he moved with astonishing grace. For a minute, she thought he was going to sweep her into his arms as he had so many times. He seemed to check his impulses abruptly and spoke a gruff greeting. He merely patted her shoulder and she felt cheated. His presence filled the room. She knew the house would feel empty when he left.

She led him to the loom and stepped back to give him room. She had removed and folded the protective sheet. Pax had made a career with his astute appraisals and uncanny assessments. She trusted his judgment implicitly, and watched the concentration in his dark eyes with respect, but also a growing apprehension.

He shook his head in disbelief. "It's weird."

"See what I mean?"

"I don't understand it at all. The first part is magnificent. But the rest . . . " His voice trailed off. "Even the selvedges are sloppy. This work is completely unlike her."

"What's happened to her? I'm scared."

"I can see why. She can't finish this as it is. It would never sell."

"And you would lose a good commission."

His chin shot up and a red flush spread across his face. "She's one of our most popular artists, but we represent a good many fine craftsmen."

She felt a pang of jealousy each time he referred to the gallery because he spoke in the plural. *Our shop . . . our artists.*

Ashamed of her outburst, she left him to get the dessert. He seemed oblivious of her as he studied each aspect of the weaving, and began to check the working mechanisms of the loom.

When she returned with pie and coffee, he was still puzzling over the weaving. Preoccupied and scarcely speaking or noticing her, he seemed unaware he had finished his pie until he put the plate back on the table. She remained silent, observing how his eyes continued to inspect Gram's work on the loom.

"Well?" she asked when she could stand the suspense no longer.

"You'll have to finish it."

"*Me?* I couldn't do that!"

"Why not? You are the only one who could."

He followed her when she stood up and walked to the loom. "Pax, I can't do it. I haven't touched yarn since I left."

His eyes expressed surprise. "You used to be a fine weaver."

"I used to be a lot of things."

"But you wrote GG about all the chic galleries in the whole area. What did you do out there, for crying out loud?"

She looked at the floor. "For starters, I didn't get married."

He jerked his attention from the loom to study her. "Neither did I," he whispered.

Tension made her cheeks burn. They stared at each other and then, each of them lowered their gaze to Gram's work. Freddie reached over to touch the bizarre swatch. "Even if I *could* finish it, which I absolutely cannot do, I'd have to get permission from Gram." She felt tears on her cheeks.

"We'd have to point out the problems and she's defensive about her art." She sniffled and he put his arm around her.

"I can't stand to hurt Gram any more." She leaned against him and he gently kissed her forehead. Her heart raced.

"You're worried and so am I – believe me, not only for my gallery. GG couldn't survive without her art."

"I know, Pax. I don't know what to do. I feel so helpless."

"We've been friends most our lives. Nothing can change that. We'll get through this because we're both committed to helping GG. I'm in this with you."

She touched his hand on her shoulder. "I don't deserve your friendship." She ran her hand up his arm, tracing the bend in his elbow. "I'm surprised that you think I could finish this. I don't have the skills. I'm not worthy to touch it."

"Hush," he said, gently. "Get a grip on yourself." He lifted her chin and touched his lips to hers. She had forgotten the warmth of a friendly kiss, and she wanted to melt into his arms. When she reached up to stroke his beard, the remembered touch of intimacy flooded her with memories, but his back stiffened and he stepped away from her.

Freddie felt a change in him as he dropped his arms. "Gotta go. But we'll think of something to do. Don't panic."

And he was gone. His rejection devastated her. He had gone back to town to someone else. Of course a man with his passion and zest for life wouldn't sit around and lick his wounds forever. He deserved better than years of loneliness, but knowing that did not make it any easier for her.

She sank down on Gram's bench and gave in to a siege of weeping. She had managed her emotions since she had come home, but a sense of worthlessness caved in on her. Guilt squeezed her heart. She was getting just what she deserved, but the pain was excruciating.

For a long time, she remained at Gram's loom. It represented the past and the future to her. She could see her grandmother leaning across the beam to shove back the beater, and hear the thumping of the loom, like a muted, continual slamming of a door. The pine walls seemed to vibrate, as though a violent windstorm had swept into the mountain valley. It spoke of all her failures and it defined the heartbreaking decline in her grandmother's health.

The problems on the loom were so obvious! *Too obvious.* Gram would never leave loose loops of yarn at the selvedge. Nor would she let discordant colors scream out to mar a lovely design. Not Gram.

And then, she understood. The errors were deliberate. They had to be. Her grandmother had purposely messed up a weaving to induce Freddie to stay home. "Why you conniving old woman! You con artist! I love you, Gram."

She told herself that for two cents she would wake her up and call her bluff. But no, she couldn't spoil Gram's fun.

A new thought rippled across her brain, and, wicked as it was, she became intoxicated with excitement. She would be a part of the subterfuge, since it was the only tie she had to Pax now. She could use it as an excuse to call him and to see him. Maybe it was unscrupulous, but she had to do *something*.

53

Freddie was surprised to find Gram at the breakfast table when she came down the next morning. After hours of sleeplessness, she had finally fallen into a troubled slumber and had overslept. She glanced around the kitchen and was glad she had washed the dishes and put the pie away last night. If Gram was aware that Pax had been there, she kept it to herself.

"I meant to get up early. Have you had your coffee, Gram?"

"Yep. You know I'm swimmy-headed until I have my liquor."

"Oh, Gram! You still call coffee your liquor?" She poured herself a cup and sat down. "I have to get a job."

"I reckon so. Call Pax."

Freddie nearly spewed her coffee all over the table. "I can't do that!"

"Why not? You loved working at Pax's gallery, land's sake!"

"Oh, Gram, I've waited four years to hear you say that."

The old lady looked confused. "That you loved working at Pax's – "

"No. Land's sake."

They laughed and Freddie grew serious. "I don't suppose you ever found any trace of that folder with your old designs."

"No. And for the life of me, I can't imagine why that stack of yellow paper is important."

"Those 'yellow papers' could be very valuable. After all, you are a famous artist and those were your earlier, original designs."

"Humph."

"But, Gram, historians are interested in that

sort of thing."

"Historians. Humph. I ain't history yet."

"Pax was going to contact the Smithsonian Institution and another famous museum up north."

Gram snorted. "Talking about working, remember there's not many around who can throw the bobbin the way you can, child. You're a fine artist. 'Course, you had the best teacher in these parts."

"You really think I'm a good weaver – or I was a good weaver?"

"You have the gift. Might be better'n me, and that's saying a lot."

"I couldn't earn a living as a weaver, Gram."

"More's the pity, land's sake."

Weave Me a Song

Chapter Six

Freddie's time in Arizona had taught her some of the hazards of trying to earn a living from weaving. Her new job would have nothing to do with the craft. But before she began job hunting, Freddie was determined to treat herself to one good hike around Gram's property.

When they were dating, she and Pax had hiked all over Avery County, climbing more than once to the top of Grandfather Mountain. They were drenched by a sudden downpour one summer afternoon, and returned home exhausted but happy. She had no time for hikes in Arizona and she had missed them.

Today the air was crisp and she felt invigorated. She could use a sweater, but she had checked the dresser drawers in her room and could not find hers. She had no idea where they had been stored. Perhaps Gram had gotten rid of them; four years was a long time to tie up space.

She paused to study the maple tree, planted

near the spot where the old oak had stood. Someone had dug a trench around it and scooped up the soil as a retaining wall to hold rain water.

Pax had said, "We planted a maple." It gave evidence of his handiwork. Next to the house, she found a neat stack of firewood and she knew that Pax had been responsible for that also. She tried to deny the possibility that he had done it to ease a guilty conscience because of the lost designs.

Gram's small farm was located at the tip of a narrow hollow and surrounded by mountains that were draped with hardwoods, pines and hemlock. Freddie studied the topography, comparing the reddish brown of Camel Back Mountain that jutted up in the middle of Phoenix to the lush greenery on Hump Back Mountain rising to the north of the property line.

Four generations of Gouges had worked this land, painstakingly clearing enough for livestock and a garden. The first families had logged the mountains and operated a small quarry where they had excavated a superior quality of granite. When the top-grade stone had petered out, a family council had closed it down as being a dangerous threat to the land.

The woods were a deep green, but here and there were round shapes where traces of orange or yellow trees were proclaiming autumn. Soon the mountains would be ablaze with reds and golds. Among the taller evergreens, the mountain ash looked squatty, pregnant with clusters of red berries. They would stand out like Christmas ornaments in a few months when the leaves of all the hardwoods had blown away. The little community, tucked in a valley between Linville and Banner Elk, was named after the mountain ash.

Across the field, she saw a sprinkling of yellow and purple – goldenrod and iron weed – making late summer appearances like costumed actors in a Broadway musical.

There used to be wild flax growing near Gram's house. Years ago, her people had raised the plant and spun their own linen. Freddie smiled when she remembered her grandmother's inheritance from *her* grandmother: a bed of madder. She had used the roots for dye making, producing pigment for colors from pink to red. She wondered where Gram's huge copper dyeing pot was.

As she walked along the property line fence that was sagging and falling, she remembered other dyes mountain folks used. Walnut hulls, roots and bark produced brown; purple was made from the pokeberry; green from green oak leaves; blue from the roots of indigo. You needed, she recalled, to dip yarn in yellow, made from the yellow coreopsis flower or the outside bark of black hickory, then indigo for some shades of green. It had always seemed strange to her, but Gram insisted that orange-yellow dye came from gray moss from an oak or apple tree. Orangy reds came from the roots of blood root, which was plentiful here. She knew that the "rock tripe" lichen produced purple and pink. She had become intrigued by color formulas early.

She turned and looked back at the house, badly in need of a paint job and new roof. The entire farm was in a state of disrepair. Beyond the house, her grandmother's chicken coop stood deserted, and the age-weathered barn was about to fall down. She knew it leaked like a sieve.

It was hard to imagine Gram without her

hens and the daily gathering of eggs. Well, she was going to get a decent job and help Gram restore the place. As soon as she earned the money she would have the unused buildings torn down and the house painted. She wanted the fence restored.

Her grandfather had kept a few livestock even after he started working in the rock quarries near Linville. Her father had maintained a fine garden, but today she couldn't tell exactly where it had been because the grounds were so overrun with waist-high weeds. For a minute, she could almost see her father weeding his plants. Freddie was in the seventh grade when he was killed.

She could not remember her mother. "Anyone who would name a helpless mountain baby a high-falutin name like 'Frederica' – why, you would know right away that they didn't belong in these parts," Gram had said. Gram's denunciation of her mother had preyed heavily on Freddie's mind while she was away. Like mother, like child? Had she inherited her mother's wanderlust, a strange addiction she would be unable to control? Would she run away again?

She wondered if, growing up alone with an older grandparent, she had failed to develop whatever skills would have allowed her to recognize the man who had taken her away for the phony he was. Obviously she had lacked the maturity to rebuff him. Guilt rose up in her mouth, scalding her throat.

Freddie's eyes swept across the valley to the towering peaks of the Blue Ridge Mountains. They were indigo-colored this morning. She caught her breath. "I will lift up my eyes until the hills. Whence cometh my help?" How many times she had heard Gram say that. She often quoted from the psalms and Freddie had accepted it without question when she was a child. Help? She stood quietly drinking in the solitude. Mountain people, isolated because of poor roads and poorer transportation, winter blizzards and other weather problems, depended heavily on their religious belief. Somewhere along the way she had ceased to appreciate her grandmother's faith, but she needed it now. The decisions she would be making in the next few weeks would have life-changing consequences.

A couple of crows flew over her, squawking a raucous welcome, breaking her trance. Nearer the house, she recognized the amiable twitters of tiny goldfinch. Their gentle chirping was one of her favorite sounds. She caught sight of them, a splash of yellow motions, and decided to buy a new thistle feeder on her next trip into town.

Freddie's gaze rose to the ridge above the property. Without warning, her mind played tricks on her as she remembered a thin, tow-headed child, in bib overalls, and a dog – always with a dog – skipping across the field to climb the rocky hillside. "Come on, Little Ree!" the child called. "Race you to the top!"

Freddie could almost see them, feel their excitement and sense of adventure. Wispy hair blew across the girl's face as she picked the small nondescript dog up and lifted him to a gray granite ledge. "Now, just hang on a minute. I'm coming around from the back. Don't got nobody to lift me up."

In a moment the child rejoined the dog and felt his wet sandpaper kisses. "Hold on, dog! Gonna knock us both off." She wrapped her arms around him and leaned her face into his fur. "Little Ree," she said, "see that last ridge over yonder? Someday you and me gonna see what's on the far side."

Little Ree strayed into their yard, a scruffy, obviously abused puppy, with a wire tied around his neck. He cowered when an adult approached him, but sidled sideways up to Freddie, wagging his tail with such vigor that he was in danger of knocking himself over. Undersized, he was white, with splotches of tan, and fur like a scouring pad.

"God only knows where that mongrel came from," Clyde said. "Or what diseases he's carrying."

"God knows that child needs a pet," his mother replied.

"Then, we'll find a decent one. I'm taking this one to the woods."

Gram reached over to restrain him. "No, son. This one might be just what she needs."

Clyde bellowed. "For crying out loud, Ma!"

"Child needs something that has had rougher treatment than she has. Poor little reject, dog is. Let it be, land's sake."

It took a couple of days before Clyde could get close enough to the dog to cut the wire that was choking him. "Yer grandma says he's a sorry reject," he said to his daughter. "She said you wanted to keep him."

"What does *reject* mean?"

"Something that's been thrown away."

"Then God threw him to me. I'll call him 'Little Reject.'"

Clyde shrugged his shoulders. "I give up."

Little Reject became a term of affection and she soon shortened it to Little Ree. Freddie had been on that very ledge the afternoon she discovered the cancerous lump behind his left ear that eventually took Little Ree's life. It seemed to her, as she reflected, that she had lost everyone she had ever loved so far – except Gram.

# # # #

Back at the house, she called to her grandmother. "I want to show you some pictures. I'll get them from my suitcase."

Gram moved over to make room for her on the couch.

"I thought you'd like to see some pictures of Indian rugs and tapestries. I have one of the looms the Navajo women use, and I brought you a small rug as a sample."

Gram went on about the lovely earth tones of the weavings, noting that, with the exception of some brilliant red and black combinations, the pictures were less vibrant than her own designs. Most of them were tan, rust and sage-green reflections of the desert. She stroked the rug example, examining the texture. "Seems heavier than my work."

Freddie shared with her what she had learned about the Navajo craftsmen, describing their upright looms and the way they sat at the base on a pile of sheepskins.

"Don't 'speck I could work on an upright loom. Must be mighty tiring, sitting on the floor. This old back couldn't manage that. You ever try one of their looms?"

Freddie shook her head.

Gram paused, then asked, "You seen my new weaving?"

"Yes," Freddie murmured.

"What do you think? Don't you care for it?"

"I especially like the color pattern, only – "

"What? Land's sake." Gram had never indicated that she cared what anyone else thought of her work. She said that she wove to the song of the artist within her. Now, her eyes darted to the loom, with all the wariness of a chickadee.

"Gram, I need you to tell me about it."

Gram slapped her hands together like a fisherman who knew the trout had taken his bait and was only waiting for the hook to be set. "I will. Later. Sometime."

Chapter Seven

Freddie had no trouble memorizing the "Help Wanted" ads in *The Avery Sentinel*. She spent the week driving up and down Highway 105 and crisscrossing Avery County, collecting job applications. She spread the papers on the dining room table, prepared a resume and started filling out forms. Her grandmother's noonday announcement dismayed her.

"Gram! What do you *mean* you invited Pax to lunch? I don't have anything to cook, my job applications are all over the table, I look a mess!" She gaped at her watch. "Why would you *do* this to me?"

Gram lifted her chin and closed her eyes. "I knew you'd accuse me of matchmaking." Piously, she explained, "I think matchmaking should be left up to the Lord and His helpers."

"And you are a divinely appointed help?" Freddie shook with frustration. "Gram, I've thrown myself at Pax ever since I got back. He's not interested. Please don't make it worse!"

Gram studied the floor and chewed on her lip. "I'm just a-praying about it, that's all. There's no law about that. And a-hoping. No law against that, either, that I know about. Now go and check the stuff in the oven. Marge fixed a chicken pie and it should be about done. You just have to finish the salad and I'll set the table."

"But my papers!"

"I can take care of that, land's sake." She leaned her cane against the table and began a neat stack of applications and resumes. "Here he is now."

Freddie, exasperated beyond measure, stomped into the kitchen and closed the door with more force than was needed. She was overwhelmed with job applications; the house was a mess; her nerves were a total disaster. Her insides churned, and her cheeks burned. Absolute helplessness tickled the back of her throat. The last time Pax had been in the house, he put his arms around her and then rejected her completely.

Marge turned from the oven to gaze at Freddie. If she recognized her vexation, she camouflaged it with a grin. She was a willing accomplice, Freddie could see.

"What are you doing here on your day off?"

The tall woman spread out her hands, palms up. "Why not? I have nothing better to do," she said. "Everything is ready and I'm going." She pulled on a gray sweater and headed out the door, only to stick her head back into the kitchen. "The peanut butter pie is his favorite."

Marge nodded toward the cabinet, then frowned and stepped back into the room. "You look just fine, honey," she whispered. "But you're as pale as dried bones. Run upstairs and slick on a little lipstick. And brush a little color on your cheeks."

Freddie's way to the stairs was blocked by Pax hunching over the table, peering over Gram's shoulder as she ran her finger down the resume. He wore a dress shirt and tie and she knew he had slipped away from the gallery. The tailored shirt emphasized his broad shoulders. His clothes contrasted, drastically, with her jeans and T shirt. She felt grimy.

"I didn't know you had earned a degree in computer science," he said over his shoulder.

"Those are my personal records." Her voice rose in a sharp crescendo. "I also learned to sling hash and pump gas in an all-night truck stop. Does that qualify me for a job – or do you need my dental records, too?" Grabbing the papers and muttering she had not expected him, she ran up the stairs.

Freddie glanced at him from the top of the stairs and saw that his lower jaw hung slack and his nose and cheeks, not covered by beard, had turned the color of a purple turnip. She almost felt sorry for him, but she was livid with her grandmother.

Pax was tossing the salad when Freddie came back to the kitchen. For a minute, she relived past lunches with Pax, sharing responsibilities and laughing over cooking mistakes. He had retained his composure. She brushed past him and grabbed a pot holder.

"Fred," he said quietly, stepping behind her, "I didn't know you weren't expecting me. I'm sorry. I don't want you to dislike me."

Completely immobilized, and with her back to him, she whispered, "I could never dislike you. I just want you to stop hating me." She was as still as a china doll. She anticipated – hoped – that he would put a hand on each shoulder and draw her back against his chest. He did not touch her.

He made a noise in his throat that was like a combination of laugh and groan. "Hate you, Fred?"

She wanted to fling the pot holder the length of the kitchen and wrap her arms around his neck. But she didn't.

In a quiet, husky voice he said, "I'll leave if you'll feel more comfortable."

"Then I'd have Gram on my back. Don't mind me. I was just immersed in my job applications."

She carefully laid the potholder down and turned to look up at him. He had reached up and loosened the knot of his tie. It was such a familiar scene that she could have described each nuance of his movements with her eyes closed. He pulled down the knot and slipped the tie over his head. He unbuttoned the top of his shirt with his left hand and draped the tie over his right shoulder. It was a scene she had remembered hundreds of times during lonely Arizona nights.

Then, nonchalantly, he picked up the salad bowl and headed for the dining room table.

The spell was broken. She felt deflated and, for a moment, slightly disoriented. She glanced around the room. What was she doing? The oven timer buzzed and she opened the door, feeling the heat on her face. Perhaps it would explain the heightened pink in her cheeks. Why was she acting like a spoiled child? She felt powerless to deal with her emotions regarding Pax.

"GG invited me to lunch often while you were away," he explained when he returned. "I usually wash the dishes. You can finish your applications."

"You'll wash the dishes! Big deal," she muttered. "Am I supposed to be impressed?"

He chortled. "Why, Fred, I didn't know I'd have to impress you." He moved to the coffee pot.

She felt heat crawling up her neck but she managed a faint smile. "I don't mean to vent my temper on you. I guess I need to apologize. I also need to thank you for watching out for Gram while I was gone."

"No sweat," he said.

She watched him open the cabinet and reach for the coffee cannister and sugar. He knew his way around Gram's kitchen better than she did.

Marge's cooking saved lunch. Freddie avoided watching Pax, but that meant she was staring at Gram. Gram seemed uncharacteristically subdued and kept glancing back and forth between Freddie and Pax.

Pax kept the conversation moving. Talking with an animation that seemed totally unlike him, he kept up a steady monologue. He brought Freddie up to date about people in the community and activities in his gallery. Slowly, she relaxed.

As she started to serve the dessert, Gram issued a plaintive plea to Pax. "Couldn't you use Freddie at the gallery?"

Freddie dropped her fork. "Gram! What has gotten into you? You planned this festive occasion just to bribe him."

Pax frowned. "Lunch with you is a bribe I would gladly accept, GG, but I just don't have any openings now." He had been talking too fast, but now earnestness gave a haltering cadence to his delivery. "Not right now. But after the wedding, Susan might want to work only part time, especially if she has a baby." He paused and smiled at Gram.

"At least that's what she says now."

Freddie heard a sharp intake of breath but she dared not look at her grandmother. When she finally glanced at her, Gram seemed to have shrunk a little. There was an expression of disbelief in her sad eyes. *So much for answered prayer,* Freddie told herself. Pax was marrying Susan.

# # # # #

Freddie accompanied Pax to the porch as she had always done during their dating days. She needed to atone for her ungracious behavior.

"By the way," he said, "I *am* impressed with your resume."

"Paxton Palmer, I didn't know I'd have to impress you."

His smile, ordinarily, would have sent her heart rollicking. "I'm sorry I don't have a place for you right now. I have a friend who was hunting someone with computer skills. Did you get an application from Bittle Plumbing? I'll call Don to see if he has hired anyone. Okay?" He took her elbow and steered her away from the door. He nodded back toward the house and asked, "Has GG shown you her weaving?"

"No. She mentioned it. I thought she might bring it up today with you."

"She was disappointed about the job."

"I'm sorry she pressured you."

He laughed. "Part of her charm is her ability to bully us all. I'll keep in touch," he said as he started down the steps, "because I may have a sale for her last wall hanging. I don't like to let her know until it's finalized. I wish you could get her to work on this one, but I am not sure she's ready."

Freddie touched his shoulder. "Wait a minute. You forgot something."

She hurried back into the house.

He stood on the lower step with a perplexed expression, and grinned when she reappeared. "Oh, my extra piece of pie! And my tie."

She handed him the pie and leaned over to slip the tie over his head and around his neck. She tightened the knot and, without realizing it, smoothed his beard as he chuckled self-consciously.

"See you, Fred. You're a wonderful cook."

"Nothing to it! Perhaps I should add 'chef' to my resume. But you know I didn't cook a thing. Marge did it all, without my knowledge. You're pretty good at washing dishes."

She watched him walk to his truck. He paused with his hand on the door to look up at her, and then he lifted his hand in a salute before he climbed into the cab. She waited until he had driven away and then the lingering sadness set in.

Lucky, lucky Susan, she whispered.

When she returned to confront Gram, she was already in bed for her afternoon nap.

# # # #

Much later she slipped into the room, remembering the hurt in Gram's eyes when Pax talked about Susan. Poor old woman. She had never lost hope that he would marry her granddaughter.

"Blew it, didn't I?" Gram asked in a tiny voice.

Freddie sorted through the blankets until she found a small hand. She lifted it to her lips and then cuddled it in her own hands. "You never blew anything in your life. You never did a thing that was not done out of love."

Gram sniffled and looked at the wall. "Why didn't Pax tell me he was courting? Oh, honey, this day must have been terrible on you."

"Gram, I deserve it. I walked out on Pax four years ago for a skunk named Brad." The stricken look in her grandmother's face broke her heart.

"Want to tell me about it?"

"I'd like to wash it from my memory forever, but I *need* to tell you." She took a deep breath. "You remember that I met Brad when he was on a buying trip for his prestigious gallery in Scottsdale – Blaylock Gallery. He convinced me that Pax was ripping us off. Said he could sell my weavings for four times what Pax was pricing them for. Promised to feature me as his 'artist in residence.' He snowed me and I fell for it, and for him."

She stood up, walked to the window and opened the shade.

"Why'd Pax let you go, I don't know."

"What choice did he have? We had already quarreled, and I guess I was on the rebound when Brad showed up."

Gram snorted and sat up. She reached behind and repositioned her pillow. "Never did like that whippersnapper. Despised him the first time you brought him home."

"Why didn't *you* stop me?"

"Didn't 'speck you to be foolish enough to run off with him. Wish to high heavens I had chained you to the bed so you couldn't go. Oh, child, I am so sorry."

"I can't blame anyone but myself. I was young and naïve, and I thought it was so romantic." She spoke in a monotone. "Brad didn't own a gallery. His uncle owned one and Brad worked for him. Mr.

Blaylock knew nothing about the 'artist in residence' program Brad described and fired him soon after I got there. What Brad did have was a wife. Conveniently forgot to mention that – or his children." She found a box of tissue and blew her noise before she could continue. "When I confronted him, he knocked me across the room. Broke my nose and then beat me black and blue. His uncle took me to the shelter and dumped me. I never even got back my samples of work."

A gasp brought her back to the chair by the bed. "Gram, I was stupid. But no one deserves that!"

Gram threw back the blankets and slipped from the bed. She knelt beside Freddie and gathered her into her arms. They wept together.

"I was too ashamed to let you know." Freddie collected her wits and stood up, lifting Gram to her feet. She felt as fragile as a baby sparrow.

Gram sank back down on the side of the bed, and Freddie lifted the old lady's feet back onto the sheet and covered her up.

"I've told you about Jill, the friend I met at the shelter. I just never told you where I met her. You know that we eventually got a little apartment together in Carefree. She was pregnant and I stayed to help her with the baby. Emily Frederica."

Gram smiled and patted Freddie's hand. "Another Frederica. Yes, you told me. I thought you met Jill in school."

"By then I felt that Pax had probably married and the best thing for me to do was to get a good education and find a decent job to support you."

"And you studied computering."

"I worked nights at any job I could find. I'd just landed a job interview for an excellent position when Pax found me. How did he find me?"

"Hired a detective. Cost him a fortune, Marge found out. Said he would mortgage his gallery if he needed to. Boy actually thought I was dying."

"Gram, you had my telephone number and post office box number. Why couldn't he find me? I didn't want you to know the conditions I was living in and I guess I was too secretive about my street address – but all you needed to do was call me."

"Foolish, foolish child. I didn't know nothing 'til I woke up in the hospital after the stroke and Pax was sitting beside me."

"Oh, no! The phone was listed in Jill's name. It didn't show up in a net search." The tears began to stream down her face again."Gram, I was horribly stupid."

"Hush, little one. You made a mistake. Seems to me we all have to take a little of the blame. But, enough. Let's make some coffee."

"But my stupidity cost me Pax."

"Appears so."

Something about the way Gram pursed her lips worried Freddie. "Gram, don't try to interfere."

"I kin pray."

Freddie smiled. "Oh, yes, Gram, you can pray. At first, I wondered why Pax gave up so easily myself." She reached for the mugs and pulled two chairs to the table. "I presumed he didn't care that much."

"Care? He moped around for months."

"He's not moping now."

"No. And that pipsqueak Susan ain't half as pretty as you." Gram stared out of the window as the coffee perked. "Once, 'fore I was married, I told your granddad that I was going to Atlanta to try to

sell my work. Read about a co-op in the catalogue."
She giggled. "Del said he would come git me if I
left. Said he would follow me. I didn't see much
sense in that, so I stayed and married him."

"And lived happily ever after."

"Yes. Del was a good man. Paxton reminds
me a lot of Del."

"Gram," Freddie pleaded, "let's forget Pax."

"I know. I know. I'll hush." Then, to herself,
she added, "Don't understand it. Don't believe it."

You had better believe it, Freddie thought, but
she kept her counsel. However, she wondered,
again, what she might have done had Pax protested
more strongly when she told him she was leaving.

It was a long time before she fell into a
troubled sleep.

# # # # #

*Her legs throbbed and terror choked her. She ran
again, but Brad gained on her. His hands were like jaws of
a vice and he was reaching for her!*

Mud and rocks impeded her flight.

*She became aware of another man and she called
out to him for help. He glanced at her as he sped by, and
she recognized him. "Pax," she screamed. "Help me!"*

She was suffocating when she heard Gram
pounding her cane on the stairs to wake her up. She
was soaked with sweat, but she felt chilled to the
bone. "It's okay, Gram. Just a dream," she called
downstairs.

They were always the same, with only slight
variations. Nightmares and visions of the shelter
would always haunt her, and she knew there would
be little sleep tonight.

Chapter Eight

In the stillness of the night, Freddie thought about the job she had been seeking in Phoenix. She wasn't in Phoenix now. She was home! Her lips slid into a smile. She did not want a job – no matter how prestigious – two thousand miles away from Gram. She would wash dishes, if necessary, to stay near the one who loved her so much.

A memory played with her mind as she lay in the dark. She was fishing with Pax in the Linville River. He had some wild notion that he could teach her to fish, but he soon gave that up. "Let me sit here and watch you," she begged him. "I love to watch you cast out into the river and to listen to the *swish* of your line."

He looked at her for a long minute, shook his head, and smiled. "Honey, just stay where I can see you; I don't care what we do as long as we're together."

She sat on a fern-covered embankment, under a canopy of lacy hemlock, listening to the river and watching Pax. She was as happy as she had ever been. When he reeled in a shiny silver mountain trout, she shouted, "Pax! I'm impressed."

She wondered if Pax remembered that today as they joked about impressing each other.

Freddie continued working on job applications. She noticed how Gram watched her with an anxious, sad look.

A telephone call came while they were still at breakfast.

"Miss Gouge? Hey. I'm a buddy of Paxton Palmer?" His voice climbed to a higher pitch at the end of each phrase, making each sentence sound like a question. "I'm Don Bittle of Bittle Plumbing? Paxton told me you would be able to set up my accounting stuff on the computer?"

Freddie smiled. "I think I could."

"I heard that works real well, and we need a better procedure? One of our competitors has his inventory on the computer, and we need to get billing and accounts receivable also? Could you come in to talk with us?"

Finally, a genuine question.

"Ten thirty?" he continued. "By the way, Paxton said you would remember my wife, Bettie Lou? She works with me?"

"Bettie Lou Wright?"

"Right? Only, she's Bittle now? I think you were in high school together?"

And so it was that, by noon, Freddie had herself a job.

#

Don Bittle was short and bald, with the exuberance and sunny disposition of a friendly puppy.

He knew as little about computers as his wife, and she boasted that her "wad of cyberspace knowledge wouldn't stuff a dead mosquito."

Seeing Bettie Lou fussing around the office brought back pleasant memories of the solicitous little mother hen who had volunteered as a surrogate nursemaid for just about the whole senior class of Ash Hill High School. Freddie was pleased to learn that the Bittles had two small sons, who were being cared for by their grandmother while Bettie Lou worked.

There was nothing auspicious about Bittle Plumbing. The store was cluttered; overstocked plumbing supplies spilled over the counters and lined the aisles. But it presented a cheerful environment and Freddie was comfortable with the setting and the personnel. The work would be challenging but she could do it. She felt a warm welcome.

Her only doubt came when she was escorted to her own office. It was neat and sparsely furnished, but the windows gave her a panoramic view of Palmer Gallery and its parking lot. Perhaps what she needed, she decided, was a daily dose of Pax to help desensitize her.

####

Freddie was so elated about the job that she decided, impulsively, to drive down to the gallery to take one last look at Gram's weaving before it was sold. She was relieved that Pax's truck was not in the parking lot. She had no idea what kind of a car Susan drove.

She took a deep breath and bravely walked up the steps. Someone had done a masterful job of designing the showroom. She had not realized before that the foyer entrance provided such a dazzling view of Gram's masterpiece. The effect was hypnotic. She paused to study it.

Gram had used all the vivid hues of the mountains and the vitality of the weaving touched Freddie's soul. Breaking with tradition, she had created a daring sweep of colors and textures that moved the eyes upward as powerfully as a mighty ocean wave. Freddie felt, looking at Gram's work, that she was on holy ground.

"Oh, Gram," Freddie whispered in hushed adulation.

Elaine had acknowledged her but had not interrupted her walk to the foot of the staircase.

"I just had to see it again, before it's removed," Freddie explained.

Elaine responded quietly. "It's hard to see it go. Like losing a good friend."

"What will you put in its place?"

"Pax has chosen a weaving by a lesser-known artist. It's quite beautiful also."

But it's Gram's place, Freddie wanted to shout.

Elaine continued. Her voice was soft, as though she were deliberately avoiding intrusion on Freddie's privacy. "Pax could have sold GG's piece several times, but he refused. He wouldn't let it go to New York or Chicago – or London. He said it belonged to this region. It's going to the Heritage Museum in Asheville. He made some lovely slides of it, and we can drive up to see it!"

"That is – good."

They stood near each other, drawn together by a mutual admiration. Serenity washed over Freddie, and she was glad she had come.

Chapter Nine

*G*ram was as tenacious as a hungry squirrel, extracting every morsel of information she could about the job. Freddie described her new employer, mimicking his eccentric speech, hiking each phrase until it was transformed into a question. "I am Don Bittle of Bittle Plumbing? My wife said you would remember her from high school? We need to set up a computer program?"

She led her grandmother through a make-believe tour of the store, kept her from tripping over the cluttered merchandise and then into her small private office. Gram was so delighted and animated that Freddie risked bringing up another subject.

She placed her hand over her grandmother's. "After I left the store, I went to the gallery to see your weaving again."

Gram remained as still and silent as though she neither felt Freddie's hand nor heard her voice. After a long moment she said, "I don't think I'll ever weave again. My hands are too arthritic. I haven't the energy to tighten the beater – or thread a bobbin."

"Not yet, but you will. There's no hurry."

"Yes, there is," Gram said, raising her chin.

"What's the hurry?"

"Pax is, that's what. He wants this weaving. Means well, I guess. Thinks I need to be 'catering to the artist' in me." She snickered. "Can't believe an old woman has earned the right to sit back and take a break."

"I'll just march in and tell him off."

Gram grinned. She reached into the pocket of her apron and pulled out a check. She carefully unfolded it and smoothed it out, running her fingers across the creased paper, then handed it to Freddie.

Freddie whistled. "When did you get this?"

"Pax was here today. Before you fuss at me, I didn't mention Susan. Nary a word 'bout her or any dad-gum wedding."

"Did you show him the weaving you left on the loom?"

"You know better than that! Anyway . . . "

"What? You owe me an explanation, Gram."

Gram twisted her apron around her hands. "I jest can't see colors like I used to."

"Don't give me that. Why did you change the color pattern?"

"Saw that? Figured it out, did you? Got your attention, didn't it?"

"It did." Freddie smiled and she heard her tone becoming less stern. "Scaring me to death. You should be ashamed, making me think you had lost your mind. I didn't realize at first that you had done it deliberately."

The old woman dropped her gaze to her

apron. "What I want is for you to finish it."

"Me?" Panic closed in on Freddie. She brought her hand quickly to her throat. "But, Gram –"

"Hush. Jest listen a bit." She took her granddaughter's hand. Gripping it in her small, cold-as-ice hands, she pled. "You know how to do the work and the treading sequence is there."

Freddie shook her head, but her grandmother continued. "Hear me out, child." Her voice faltered. Her eyebrows lifted and her face became mobile, cheeks rippling into little humps, and mouth curving into an emotional appeal. "I need to hear the music of my loom."

"You'll weave again, Gram."

Gram stood up. To Freddie, she seemed to have shrunk a couple of inches. "You don't understand. These twisted limbs and tired shoulders – I need to leave the weaving to you."

Gram's skin was flushed with a bluish tinge and Freddie thought she might faint. Freddie knew she was trapped. "I'll try, Gram," she whispered.

A glimmer of hope lit Gram's washed-out eyes. Freddie followed the stooped figure into the living room.

Leaning on her cane, Gram attempted to balance herself, trying to flip the sheet off the loom. She winced, dropped her cane and grabbed her wrist.

Freddie picked up the cane and undraped the loom to study the work. She laughed, unexpectedly. "You were pretty obvious. I don't remember that you ever messed up a design before."

"Never needed to, 'fore now. Well, pamper your Gram. See what you recollect."

The animal smell of home-dyed wool was

missing; the cotton scent was bland in comparison. Freddie hesitated before she eased herself onto Gram's bench and slid gingerly across to position herself at the loom. She lightly touched the foot pedals with the tip of her toe; testing, exploring as warily as though she were seated at the console of a mighty pipe organ and her foot, sweeping across the pedals, could evoke a powerful cacophony.

Stroking the smooth wood of the beam, worn into a satiny finish, she was hesitant. She ran her fingers over Gram's "draft" neatly taped to the top of the loom. With a touch of reverence, she lifted the beater and shoved it back as far as it would go. She adjusted the tension of the weft with her right foot brake.

She took a deep breath before she met her grandmother's eyes. Freddie felt a strange calming effect as she brought her attention back down to the weaving. "I'll have to undo several rows," she said in a small voice.

Gram nodded.

Freddie picked up the boat-shaped shuttle and examined it. She cradled the shuttle in her hand, caressed the polished wood with her thumb. Gram had said she had cut her teeth on it, but it felt unfamiliar, foreign in her palm. "Four years. It's been four long years," she whispered.

She ran her hands along the beam, tested the warp threads with her fingertips and that touch revived a craving and activated a transfusion of confidence and a tiny tingling of enthusiasm. She nodded at Gram.

She cautiously threaded the shuttle between the warp threads, and holding her breath, pushed it back toward the left of the loom. Gram patiently watched as she reached between the threads to nudge it along. At first her movements were faltering and laborious. She stuck the tip of her tongue between the lips in the corner of her mouth and concentrated as Gram gently coached and encouraged her. She undid the erratic work, and they giggled over the bizarre choice of colors.

As simple as the task was, the idea of undoing Gram's work was draining and she was worn out by the time she had worked back down to the original design. Gram helped her rewind the bobbin with gray thread and fit it back into shuttle.

"You're tired, child. Best stop tonight."

"I've got to see if I can do it. Only a little bit more, Gram."

Her grandmother had said she could throw a shuttle with the best of weavers, but today her attempt was anemic, without enough inertia to send it through the loom. She had to reach through the threads and retrieve it. She threw it again, putting more force in the arm motion. This time she was successful. She caught the shuttle with her left hand. Her shoulders relaxed ever so slightly.

"Got it!" Gram exclaimed.

"No, but I will."

Slowly, Freddie began to perfect the three basic motions: throwing the shuttle; treadling with her feet to change the sequence in Gram's pattern; pulling back the beater to lighten the weft. She was drawing from some ancestral need. Was it the desire to create that ran through her veins? Excitement quickened her heart, and she felt renewed.

Gram stopped her. "You're plum tuckered out and you have a new job to go to tomorrow. Time to stop, child."

Freddie had not realized how tense she was until she started to leave the loom. "It'll take a while to learn how to do it again."

"But you'll do it. Got talent, the child has, I always said."

Freddie knew, as she climbed the stairs, that as weary as she was, the nightmare that sometimes invaded her sleep would not bother her tonight.

Chapter Ten

*W*ork, she hoped, would provide an escape. She would not have time to think about Pax, or Susan. However, Susan called twice during Freddie's first week at work. She left a message on the machine, but Freddie conveniently "forgot" to return the call. When Susan phoned to invite her to lunch, Freddie begged off, pleading the horrendous task of setting up a new program.

Friday Freddie glanced up to see Susan standing in her office doorway. Her hair was the color of apricots and her eyes sky blue. She was tall and slender and attractive with a refreshing lack of pretense. She looked momentarily disconcerted until Freddie, realizing she was scowling at her visitor, forced a smile.

"Greetings, Frederica!" Susan's voice was melodic. "I had to stop by the store anyway, so just thought I'd say Hi."

"Hello." Freddie's response was as flat as a river rock.

Susan stood on first one foot, then the other. She seemed about to burst with news. "I wanted to invite you and GG to the wedding."

"Wedding?" Freddie could not breathe. She wanted to despise the radiant Susan, but her breathless effervescence threw Freddie off balance. Music drifted down the hallway, a guitarist strumming the chords to "Softly and Tenderly" on Bettie Lou's gospel radio station. Freddie's throat tightened.

"The wedding isn't for months yet, but there's so much planning to do, and showers, and picking out china and things. I just wanted to get it on your calendar."

"Calendar?" A small squeak slipped from constricting throat muscles.

Susan seemed oblivious of her lack of enthusiasm. She chatted cheerfully. "You know, we're going to be neighbors."

This could not be happening. "Neighbors?" A weariness in her neck and shoulders spread down her arms and her hands felt heavy. She looked down at her computer keyboard.

Susan's voice quavered with uncertainty and when Freddie looked up, a quizzical expression lifted her eyebrows. "Didn't Pax tell you?"

Taking a deep breath, Freddie finally managed six consecutive words. "He said you were getting married."

Susan hesitated. "I had to pick up some supplies for Eddie," she seemed distracted, "and thought I'd drop in for a moment." Her enthusiasm wound down, slowly, like the spinning of a toy top. She apologized for interrupting and turned to flee.

Bewildered, Freddie asked, "Who's Eddie?"

"My fiancé. Eddie Miller. I just assumed that

Pax had told you we're building our new house out on Turkey Hollow Road, just below GG's property."

Freddie felt a little dazed. "You're marrying Eddie Miller and you're going to live on Turkey Hollow Road?"

"Yes."

"Are you sure?"

Susan looked startled. "I think so." Then, suspiciously, "Do you know something that I don't?"

Freddie laughed. Susan looked skittish, eyes darting around the office. She jumped when Freddie abruptly stood up.

Freddie gestured a sweeping invitation with her arm. "Come in," she invited belatedly. Susan glanced into the hallway.

"I'm sorry," Freddie confessed. "My mind was a thousand miles away. I wasn't thinking about the wedding. Please. Tell me all about it!"

"Don't you remember Eddie? He was two years ahead of us in school. In Pax's class." Susan scooted to the chair in front of the desk. "He keeps insisting on a small wedding; he's so shy. But I want the whole shooting match with bridesmaids and everything."

"Of course you do, Susan. Do you have time for a lunch break?" She hoped she didn't sound condescending.

####

Freddie broke the news to her grandmother. "Gram, do you know an Eddie Miller?"

Gram pursed her lips and remained in deep thought. "That must be the nice boy who helped Pax clean up the rubbish of the oak tree when it fell during the blizzard."

"Did you know he was the one building the new house on Turkey Hollow Road?"

"Don't think I did. That's nice."

"He's getting married. We're invited to the wedding."

"That's nice, but I haven't been going out much. How come he invited us?"

"Bet you don't know who he's marrying," Freddie teased.

"My! Ain't you full of gossip tonight!"

"Susan Deerfoot came to see me. Gram, Susan is marrying Eddie. They'll be our neighbors."

Gram's eyebrows arched. "But I thought Susan was marrying Pax." Then, she grinned – a wide, big split in her tiny face, from earlobe to earlobe.

Freddie explained, "Do you realize that Pax never said *he* was marrying Susan, only that she was getting married."

Gram snorted and gave her an impish smile, and emitted an unladylike cackle. "See? See? Told you I'd pray!" She astonished Freddie by hooking her cane over her arm and dancing a little jig. "Hallelujah! Praise the Lord!"

Freddie tried to calm her. "I hate to burst your bubble," she said with a hand on Gram's shoulder, "but I know there's someone. There has to be. Maybe he's in love with Elaine."

"Hope not. Elaine has a nice husband."

For a split second, Freddie's heart soared – until she remembered the tension in Pax the evening he drew back from her. "That doesn't mean he's interested in me, Gram."

"Then that's your problem, my child."

"What do you mean 'my problem' and what in tarnation am I supposed to do? I've made a fool out of myself already, throwing myself at him."

Gram's response was like a cold slap in the face. "How's about forgiveness?"

"What do I have to forgive him for?"

"Ain't talking about him. You."

Freddie gasped. "Me?"

"Yep. It's *you* you can't forgive. It's a-churning in you – the anger's a-eating your insides out. You plum scare him off."

Freddie was sick then – sick at her stomach and sick all the way through her body. She had to go upstairs. But, Gram was right and she knew it. She didn't know, however, if she could ever forgive herself. She remembered a scene in Arizona in the shelter, when a group of women were sitting around, venting their rage.

"All men are rotten," one woman said. "You can't trust a single man."

Freddie interrupted. "I've known three good men. My father, my granddad and Pax." She told them about Pax.

"And you think you can really trust him?" her questioner asked.

"With my life."

There were a few caustic remarks and laughter and then one woman stated, "But not with your worldly goods."

"With anything. Everything."

"Then, what in God's earth are you doing in a woman's shelter in Phoenix, Arizona, for crying out loud?"

"Because I'm a fool." And she knew it was true. She had thrown him away.

####

It was getting harder and harder to run. He was gaining on her and the throbbing ache in her legs shrieked out to stop, but she fled for her life. Searing anguish whipped through her body and made her stumble. She could feel the heat from his breath and a terror that was black and horrible clutched at her throat.

The other man nodded at her, smiled at her, and ran on.

She awoke before Gram pounded on the stair and lay still, waiting for any sound indicating that she had disturbed her grandmother. Perhaps she had not screamed out tonight.

She turned toward the window. It would be many hours until the first touch of sunrise, but she knew she would be awake to see the palest eastern light in the black sky.

Chapter Eleven

In the days that followed, Freddie worked herself into a frenzy at the office and at home to make time to get to the loom at night. As she finally slid onto the bench after supper each evening, she had to readjust her whole mode of activity and deliberately curtail her hectic pace. The weaving process was slow and tedious to a body no longer accustomed to its special tensions, and by the time she stopped at night her shoulders and back ached.

Gram had bragged that her loom was wise and seasoned. Freddie was counting on it; she needed all the help she could get. She told her grandmother that she had forgotten more than Freddie would be able to learn. The struggle to get back into the rhythms was arduous, but she was grateful for the fascination that the work had become to her. It insulated her from the pain in her life.

Gradually, the weaving became automatic and the allure of the loom took over. The beauty of Gram's design; the simplicity of the operation; the immediacy of the response of the loom and the smooth, rhythmic motion gave her sheer pleasure. The problems and concerns of the world receded as she worked. The pride in artistry had been passed down to her from generation to generation. Her great-grandmother's aspiration to attain excellence had been as strong as her own.

She smiled as she slipped away from the loom, and started stiffly up the stairs. She stepped back down to kiss her grandmother's cheek. She knew her shoulders would be sore in the morning, but an incredible sense of achievement accompanied her up to bed.

One afternoon, something blocked the late evening light in the window and she looked up to see Pax standing on the porch. "What are you doing, window peeking?" she called.

Deep laughter rumbled from his thick chest, and she felt herself go weak. "I didn't know you were weaving again. Are you as mean as your grandmother, or will you let me see what you're doing?"

"I'm a lot meaner, but come in." She hoped her voice was steady. He was in casual slacks and a plaid shirt. She noticed he wore no tie.

He pushed open the screen door and she felt the floor vibrating as he walked into the room to stand beside her to look at the weaving. "I've been standing outside, listening to the loom. You have the rhythm down pat. You've been practicing."

She brushed her fingers through her short blonde hair and raised anxious eyes to his face.

He smiled. "Fred," he said, "you're going to be as good as she is."

"But it's her design. I can't create one like this." She paused in her work and pushed up the sleeves of her lavender sweater. "She finally explained to me about messing up the weaving."

"Then it *was* deliberate. I thought it must be."

"She messed it up just to scare me to death and to make me stay home."

His sudden laugh was mischievous. "I'll have to figure out some way to scare you and keep you home." He was tormenting her. She felt a flush start at her neck and climb up to her ears. "So, otherwise, how are you doing?"

"Fine. Thanks for recommending me to Don. I like the office crew."

"The question man? He brags on you? He says you and Bettie Lou get along famously?"

She laughed and automatically checked the tension on her warp. She laid down the shuttle and started sliding across the bench to climb down.

"Don't stop. I didn't come to bother you. I came to see GG."

"Oh." Her face must have shown her disappointment.

"That's not what I mean, Fred!"

"Gram's in the kitchen." She changed positions and moved back to the middle of the bench.

He reached over and took her hand. "Please, let's not quarrel. Come with me. I need to talk with both of you." Without a word, she slid toward him.

"What I came for," he said as they made their way through the house, "is to invite GG and you to Asheville, Saturday. The leaves will be at their peak. We can drive down the Parkway and enjoy the scenery. I want to see how the museum is displaying her work. I've heard rumors that I want to confirm."

####

"Oh, my! " Freddie sighed with pleasure. "Look at the reds and the yellows. Like melted gold. Autumn has never been more shimmeringly spectacular, or the air more crystal clear and sparkling."

Pax chortled. "Fred, your description, never mundane, has escalated to hyperbole. Shimmeringly spectacular? Sparkle? Air can't 'sparkle'."

"It does today," she countered.

"Sparkle? It's crisp and it's clear and it's nippy. But it doesn't sparkle. *You* are sparkling!"

"Women can't sparkle," Gram said from the back seat. "Only diamonds or lakes or ice crystals sparkle. Del used to bring me icicles. Now, *icicles* sparkle."

Pax gave Freddie a smile that was comradely and private, as Gram continued her rambling.

"Sunlight touches an icicle and it looked like thousands of tiny lights. Del couldn't afford no diamonds, but I kept his icicles in a vase on the back porch most of the winter. Said, he did, they were a poor man's diamonds."

"Okay," Pax conceded. "Air, women, lakes, diamonds, icicles – no matter! The day is a fine one and even the Parkway isn't too crowded this early in the morning."

He had picked them up before eight, driving a large, comfortable sedan. "Where's the Bullet?" Freddie asked, enjoying using the nickname for his truck, but just a bit disappointed.

"This is a business trip, in a way, since we are checking on our work at the museum, so I borrowed my partner's car. The truck would be too hard on GG."

Gram said, "Wal, I declare. I could of had Marge pack a lunch."

Pax smiled. "The trip to the museum is business, GG. Lunch will be pleasure. My pleasure. It's been a long time since I took two beautiful ladies to lunch."

"Go on with you," Gram said and insisted on climbing into the back seat. She had tried to beg out of going, reminding them that she had gone nowhere since her illness. Pax had talked her into the trip by promising to stop by an apple farm on the way home.

"I can't pick no apples today."

"You can sit in the car and drink hot apple cider while Fred and I pick apples."

They wound down the short twisting drive from the Blue Ridge Parkway to the Mountain Heritage Museum. Their banter, so full of laughter and teasing all morning, became hushed as they approached the building.

Pax led the way and when they entered the room featuring mountain art, he strode ahead to locate Gram's work, allowing them to follow at a more leisurely pace. They saw him stop, lift his eyes and turn to beckon to them. They clustered together at the base of a magnificent exhibit. Freddie stopped dead, standing with rapt, spell-bound attention. Gram stepped back, and Pax placed a hand on her shoulder to steady her. She braced herself against the ramrod-straight Pax. He put his arm around each woman and they stood wordlessly, as one unit.

"Extraordinary," Pax whispered finally breaking the spell. "Inspiring."

"Humbling." Gram said.

Freddie was speechless. She leaned to Pax.

Even with Pax's imposing statue, they were dwarfed by the high ceilings. It's like a cathedral, almost hallowed, Freddie thought.

They stared at Gram's wall hanging and in this setting, it was as though none of them had seen it before. Soft lights washed the weaving as it hung alone on the white wall, the singular display.

"It's a masterpiece," Freddie said, her voice breaking. "And it belongs in this exact place." Her face contorted with emotion, but neither of her companions noticed.

They might have remained rooted to the spot indefinitely, but Gram began trembling and together they edged toward the entrance, too caught up in the moment to continue the tour. Freddie had forgotten how weak her grandmother was.

Pax hesitated. "I wanted to introduce you to the curator."

"Another time, please?" Gram asked and her voice was little more than a quiver.

Freddie nodded mutely. This special time should be theirs alone.

Chapter Twelve

"*A*re you sure, GG, that you are not too tired to stop by the apple farm? " Pax snatched an anxious glace at his backseat passenger. She leaned against the pillows and her face was ashen. Lunch had failed to revive her.

"Wal, I hope not. Didn't come this far just to gape at a swatch of yarn nailed to the wall. 'Course I want to stop."

"Swatch of yarn! It that all you think of it?" Freddie was indignant.

Gram chuckled. "No, it's not. I'm right smart proud of the thing."

"You should be, GG. But I'll need another for my gallery."

"My granddaughter is working on it."

Freddie turned to Pax. "I have a confession." She reached over and laid a hand on his arm and noticed that he did not flinch as he had her first night home. "I got angry when Elaine said you had turned down buyers in New York and Chicago."

"And London. That was really difficult. But I will have to scold Elaine for telling you that. It was privileged information," he teased.

"London? Someone wanted to buy my weaving and take it all the way to England?" Gram came alive. "How come? And why didn't you sell it?"

"I think, as your agent, I have that prerogative. I thought it was in the best interest of my client and her fans to place it where we could enjoy it."

"You found the perfect place for it. Right, Gram?"

"Don't know what all the fuss is about. Just a dumb old hanging."

The small orchard draped over the hillside like a crocheted afghan. The gnarled trees looked like textured needlework. Their crooked branches made them seem hundreds of years old, and indeed, some of them approached that mark.

Pax set Gram up with a mug of aromatic apple cider and her pillows, and cautioned Freddie to get her jacket. "It's beginning to get pretty cool." Grabbing two plastic buckets, he led Freddie down the narrow road into the sun-splashed orchard. The hum of bees muted traffic sounds on the parkway.

"The owner told me there were only a few good ones still left on the trees, but we should be able to fill these." He led her far from other pickers. She felt light-headed, exhilarated with the beauty, the scent of the ripe fruit, the mountains rising around them.

"Remember," Pax said, "the time we took that new boy – Harvey Winchester, I think – to the pumpkin patch and made him think we were going to steal all the pumpkins for the school's Halloween party?"

"It was the Wright's pumpkin patch. I'd forgotten all about that!" She giggled.

"Bettie Lou and her brother were in on the joke until she felt sorry for Harvey and confessed."

"She was already acting as a little mother hen to everyone."

Freddie reached up to pick her first apple and her fingertips just grazed the bottom of the fruit. She jumped to grab it. The ripe fruit escaped from her fingers and went tumbling down the hill as she raced to retrieve it. She felt like a kid again.

Pax's laughter was buoyant. "No, Fred. Like this!" He plucked one and dropped it into the bucket, dramatically. "Pick one. It's easy."

"Oh, sure! Pick one!" She stretched to her tiptoes. "What? Do you think I'm some grasshopper?"

Weak with laughter, he stumbled and nearly fell. "I never saw a grasshopper with blonde curls bouncing up and down."

He put his hands around her waist and lifted her to within easy reach of the branches. He seemed to hold her effortlessly and she felt the strength as he gripped her waist.

"That's more like it."

He sat her on his shoulders, and she picked several applies and slid them into the bucket with the delicacy of handling dynamite. The odor of fermenting fruit was rife, but it was his closeness that produced intoxication.

"Am I heavy?"

"About as heavy as any other grasshopper."

She dusted a green apple on her denim jacket sleeve and pressd it against his lips as he held her. He chomped on it as he eased her slowly down, holding her close, clutching her against him. She sensed his reluctance to release her. She leaned toward him, brushing her cheek on his beard and she laughed. "You tickle."

He'd been the love of her life once and she had destroyed the relationship. guilt and shame flooded her being. She was afraid he would recognize her yearning. She felt vulnerable and exposed.

He eased her feet to the ground and too quickly, she stepped away from him. "You'll get sick on green apples," she quipped, disconcerted, trying to hide her turmoil.

"You only get sick on stolen ones. We'll pay for these."

"Pax . . ."

"What, honey?"

She shook her head and shrugged her shoulders. "Oh, I don't know, but . . .This is the happiest day I can remember. Thank you for bringing us."

"Fred, we'll have many happy days." A breeze swept up the mountain and it blew his brown hair, swirling it lightly, giving him a sudden boyish look.

"You're too good to us," she said and moved further away from him.

His smile vanished. He looked perplexed. "You're confusing. Do you know that?"

She arched her eyebrows. "Because I say you are good to Gram and me? I don't deserve it."

"Don't deserve what?" he asked impatiently. "Friendship – and love – is not based on merit! What's wrong with you? Are you going to spend the rest of your life fighting me, doing some idiotic penance?"

"Fighting you?" She dropped her gaze and poked at an apple with the toe of her shoe. "It's more than that, Pax. You know it is more than that."

"I don't know anything. Are you going to

explain to me? Can't you trust me?"

"How can *you* trust *me*? That's the question." She continued quietly, "My mother ran away."

"So? What's that got to do with anything? You're not making sense, Fred."

"But I ran away, too."

"You came back."

"So did my mother – several times – before she left for good. She was just my age and Gram thinks I'll do the same. It's probably a heredity thing."

She was crying now, and he dropped the buckets of apples and folded her into his arms. "Fred," he whispered – just "Fred."

Gently he lifted her chin and caressed her face, her eyelids and her lips.

She felt all wobbly as he kissed the top of her head and held her tightly. She wanted the rest of the world to go away.

"You are not your mother, sweetheart. You're not anything like her, and what she did has nothing to do with you."

"I can't explain the first time I ran away. Gram says that – "

"Fred. Hush! GG is wise and she is wonderful, but she is not always right. Is that all that's bothering you?"

"I hurt you once, Pax. And Gram. I'd never forgive myself – "

He lifted her chin, and in the warmth of his kisses it seemed to her, that for the moment, the world had gone away. They lingered until the shadows painted the grass gray under the trees and the air grew chilly, as he cuddled her in his strong arms.

Gram was dozing when they returned to the

car. They loaded the apples into the trunk and started the car before she stirred. Freddie averted her face from her grandmother, hoping the signs of tears would be gone by the time they arrived home.

####

They could see the red, white and blue express mail envelope tucked in the screen door as they drove up the driveway. Freddie was puzzled until she pulled it out and found that it was from her friend Jill.

"I wonder what's wrong," she said. The paper tab tore in her hand, and Pax handed her his pocket knife. Her hands trembled and he took the knife back and slit the letter open. He studied her with concern.

Freddie pulled out several sheets of paper and began reading. "Would you believe it? That job I was applying for in Phoenix is making an offer without the second interview. They're offering me three times what Don can pay me!"

Pax whistled, and gathering up the bags of apples, he brushed past her. "Where do you want these, GG?"

"Three times!" Enunciation slurred with excitement, she struggled to steady the rising pitch in her voice. "That would pay rent on a nice apartment – and decent child care. I'm supposed to call either their office or Jill right away." She was hardly aware of the puzzled expression in Pax's eyes but later, it would haunt her.

"Three times what I'm making! I have to call her now. Excuse me, I have a telephone call to make!" She squeezed between Pax and Gram and reached for the telephone.

The call took longer than she had expected and there was lots of chattering with Jill. She had to talk with Emily also. When the put the phone down, Pax was gone.

Gram looked worried. "What did you tell Jill?" she asked.

"To apply for the job herself."

Gram's face broke into a broad grin. "You won't take it?"

"It would be quite a commute. Where's Pax?"

"He left." Her voice was solemn.

"I don't understand why he would leave so quickly. He didn't even say goodbye."

"I think he thought you were taking the job," Gram said. "He looked like he lost his best friend. Just shrugged his shoulders and shot outta here."

It was as though someone had kicked her in the pit of her stomach. "Oh, Gram! Surely no, Gram!" The joy drained from her and she felt wretched.

Chapter Thirteen

Never in her life had she felt so desolate. She had dared to share her most profound self-doubts with Pax. He comforted her, reassured her and then assumed, after all, that she was going to walk out on Gram – and him.

For the first time in the whole long set of weird circumstances, she didn't blame herself. But shifting the responsibility didn't relieve her pain. It intensified it, making her feel utterly helpless. She had allowed herself to become vulnerable again.

After a sleepless night, she dragged herself downstairs. She usually found Gram in pre-dawn hours, sitting next to the window, nursing a cup of boiled coffee, holding the mug with both hands. Today Gram was busy in the kitchen and Freddie smelled country ham and homemade biscuits.

"Gram? What are you doing in the kitchen so early in the morning?"

"Land's sake, child, you've cooked breakfast for me all these weeks, and I sorta thought you might need a little propping up today. And you do. You look as spiritless as a winter salamander."

Ordinarily, Freddie would have enjoyed Gram's simile. She merely nodded this morning. If a hibernating salamander lacked any zest for living, she fit that description. "Is it that obvious?"

"Plum pitiful, you are. Child, you'd have to reach up to touch bottom." Gram scurried to pour her coffee.

"I wish I'd never met Pax Palmer."

"Nah, you don't. Want gravy on this biscuit?"

"I'm sorry you went to so much trouble. I don't think I can eat a thing."

Gram scrunched up her nose. "Wal, try."

Sitting at the table, Freddie stirred her coffee. She didn't have the energy to argue, but she found comfort in the unexpected reversal of morning roles.

"Reckon it was hard on the man. He heard you talking about child care, and a nice apartment. Maybe you should call him."

Freddie gasped. "Child care! But he knew I was talking to Jill!"

"I don't know what the man was thinking. In fact, I learned long ago that I couldn't be sure about what my Del was thinking, let alone any other man."

"That's the silliest thing I ever heard. You could read Granddad like a book. I have tried to call Pax. All I get is the stupid answer machine and he won't return my calls."

There was a long pregnant silence and when she broke it, Gram's voice held a quality of sadness Freddie had never heard before. "No, I couldn't read him all the time. Once . . . "

Freddie put down her cup. "Don't tell me

you two had a fight. I don't believe it."

"Not a fight. That would have been better. Could have cleared the air. We just lost it once. Our love 'bout got buried under, and I didn't even realize it. Weren't my fault, or his neither, but . . . "

"Tell me, Gram."

# # # #

It was after a dazzling fall that diphtheria put Garnet Gouge in bed and took the life of her three-year-old daughter, Lenore. She could remember, only vaguely, family and neighbors drifting in and out of her house and Del standing beside the bed, a solemn shadowy figure.

The pattern of daylight and darkness blurred until only a drab grayness remained. She became aware that the house was still – neighbors and their casseroles and cakes were gone. A sadness permeated the rooms like winter cold and she wondered if Del had failed to properly bank the fireplace.

She woke up, weeks later, to find that the baby furniture and toys had been removed. She was inconsolable with grief. At first, Del tried to comfort her, but she could not respond. He lay in bed, on his back, arms rigid at his sides and she curled up on her left side, away from him. Night after night, she cried herself to sleep as he stared at the ceiling.

Mountain women could ill afford to wallow in grief, so she finally got out of bed and went through the motions of housework. Del had to go back to work. An unbearable emptiness threatened to destroy their marriage.

They talked little and quarreled only once – when she wanted to sell her loom. He would not hear of it. The void between them grew abysmal.

One January night, waking up to discover the bed empty, she called his name and grabbed her robe. From the kitchen, she could see the barn door – a dark void in the moonlight, and a sickening fear gripped her. If he had taken the truck and left her, she could not blame him.

She grabbed her worn work jacket and pulled on her boots. Taking no time to hunt a flashlight, Garnet stumbled through falling snow to the barn. The truck was there and behind it, she could see lights in the storeroom. She had not been in the building in months and, although she had never asked, she knew that Lenore's things were stored there.

She was startled by the sound of sobbing. She had never heard a man cry before, and she was terrified as she slipped furtively to the doorway of the storeroom. Del was sitting on the floor, his long legs pulled up to his chest. In the murky light, he rocked the hand-hewn cradle he had made for Lenore. Garnet had never in her life witnessed a scene of such total desolation.

"Del – ?"

He jerked forward and swiped at the tears on his face. "What are you doing here?"

She was startled by the gruffness in his voice. She had not meant to snoop, but she couldn't leave him in such agony and stepping closer, she wordlessly caressed his shoulder.

"You'll catch cold," he said.

She knelt beside him and pulled a rag from her pocket and wiped his cheeks. He took her hand in his and pulled it to his lips, and his cheeks contorted with pain.

"I didn't know you were hurting so much," she whispered.

"I promised you a house full of young'uns."

She pulled his face to her, wrapped her arms around him and rocked him back and forth, her heart breaking. It was several minutes before the silence calmed her and she realized he had stopped crying.

Del took the damp rag from her and dabbed at her checks. He confessed quietly, "When I lost my baby, I lost you, too, Garnet."

"You ain't agoin' lose me. Might wish you could, sometimes."

"Hush," he said, clutching her tightly.

####

Freddie sighed and studied her hands. She felt as though she had been eavesdropping on a private and precious moment in Gram's memory.

Her grandparents had never been demonstrative in front of others. Their affection was evidenced by voice tone. She always referred to him as "My Del." He called her "Precious Garnet" and raised her gemstone name to jewel status.

Gram brushed at her cheeks with the palm of her hand, as a child might do. She looked as though she might fade away.

"Gram?" It seemed intrusive. "Are you all right?"

Gram jerked her head up. "Appears to me that Pax is made of the same kind of stuff your Grandpa was. He'll come around, God willing."

"I haven't the strength to debate it, Gram," she said. The words that crushed her spirit were an echo from Pax. "GG is wise, and she's wonderful, but she's not always right."

Weave Me a Song

Chapter Fourteen

The aroma of apples, simmering away on the stove, greeted Freddie when she returned from work. Marge stirred her bubbling homemade apple sauce and Freddie knew she would never smell, see, or taste an apple again without a tinge of sadness.

Sadness was not a part of Gram's makeup this afternoon. She was vibrant with excitement. "I'm going to the gallery tomorrow," she explained. "Susan is coming to get me right after lunch and you can pick me up after work."

"What's going on?"

"Oh, it's just a craft fair committee meeting. But, you needn't worry. Pax is out of town so you won't bump into him."

She was elated to see her grandmother so happy, but a little sad that she had so completely accepted that Pax was out of her life.

####

Freddie drove into the gallery parking lot, and wound around the cars parked in the front lot to a spot near the river. She paused to admire the profile of Grandfather Mountain. This view made it easy to identify the forehead, chin and nose of the old fellow, looming directly behind the gallery. The Linville River, edged with granite boulders and hardwood trees, dressed to the hilt in apricot autumn finery, seemed to wrap around the north side of the building, incorporating it unobtrusively into the picturesque setting.

For a business with so much going on, the gallery appeared surprisingly unattended. She saw no one when she stepped into the foyer. Immediately, she raised her eyes to the landing where Gram's weave had hung and, frowning, hurried toward the staircase.

The weaving that had replaced Gram's was certainly striking. This must be the 'beautiful piece by a lesser known artist' that Elaine had spoken about. It was in soft hues of blue, green and mauve with a landscape, a woven view of the Blue Ridge Mountains, inserted in the pattern.

It was similar to one she had done years before, when she had experimented with a new tapestry technique. Moving toward the landing, she saw the small inscription: *"Majesty* by Frederica Gouge. For Display Only. Not for Sale."

Stunned, she gawked at the exhibit. She remembered how she had given the piece to Pax as a Christmas gift. She had not named it and had, indeed, forgotten all about it. It had been at least five years since she had completed the design. Even though it was her own work, she was delighted by its beauty. She savored a taste of pride and also one of astonishment. She wondered if other artists were overwhelmed by seeing their work dramatically displayed in so elegant and imposing a manner.

Susan called to her from the other wing of the gallery and she hurried to join the small group of artists who were planning the fair. Walking across the showroom, she was dizzy with the realization that her work was part of this kaleidoscope of colors, textures and beautiful shapes.

The renovation of the gallery had included a small conference room and it was here that she found her grandmother and eight or ten other artisans. In the company of her fellow artists, Gram seemed to have experienced a rebirth. Her shoulders were straight, her eyes danced with excitement. "Come, set, child, and have some hot apple cider. Pour her a cup, please, Elaine."

No one seemed to notice she referred to her adult granddaughter as "child" or that she was giving crisp orders to one of the owners of the gallery.

Two men jumped to offer their seats. "So, we finally get to meet GG's granddaughter!" One of them said and the other raved about her weaving on display in the showroom.

Freddie felt a rush of pleasure and knew she was blushing. She wrapped her hands around the pottery mug of the pungent hot drink. There was a camaraderie among this group that was as refreshing as the spice aroma swirling out of her mug, pushing aside her reservations about the scent of apples. "I'm surprised that you actually use these gorgeous handmade mugs," she said to Elaine.

"'Course she does," replied a man who called himself Durrell. "I made them to use in here."

"GG says you'll be able to demonstrate weaving on her loom at the fair," Elaine said, pulling out a chair next to her and easing into it.

Ten minutes ago, Freddie would have protested. Still on a high from seeing her work displayed and finding the joy in Gram's eyes, she nodded.

Her acceptance was all Elaine was waiting for and she quickly dismissed the meeting. Freddie found herself enveloped by friends of her grandmother as each of them came by to introduce themselves. Some she remembered, but others had become friends since she had gone away.

"I tried to buy one of your gram's pieces years ago," a distinguished looking gentleman said, "I drove by her place and saw some rugs hanging on the porch railing, and I just stopped right then and walked up the steps and knocked on her door. She said she didn't sell her work but offered to give me one. I was a stranger! Can you believe that? I was a stranger and she was going to give me something she had worked a long time on. We worked out a deal. I carved her a bread bowl and she gave me a rug. Still have it, too."

Gram beamed. "I was right surprised, Albright, and I have the bowl, too. That was 'fore I even thought about selling anything. Anyhow, those first rugs were made out of torn up old clothes." She laughed as though she had played a fine joke on the old man.

A white-haired woman, no bigger than a minute, leaned toward Freddie. "I'm demonstrating candlemaking at the fair. I love weavings, and Mr. Palmer explained all about your work, *Majesty*, to me. But he won't sell it.

"He will not sell it." She pounded the table with her fist for emphasis. "I can remember when you could drive through these parts and see colorful quilts or blankets hanging on clothes lines or fences everwhere for sale."

Susan refilled Freddie's mug. "Did you ask Mr. Palmer why he refused to sell that weaving, Mrs. Olson?" She winked at Freddie, causing an uneasiness to flutter her heart.

Mrs. Olson looked perplexed. "Yep. As a matter of fact, I did ask him. Blame if I remember what he said." She laughed and was answered by amiable chuckles from others enjoying the good-natured way she joked about her memory.

Freddie watched a little coterie of craftsmen hover around her grandmother. She was grateful for the obvious respect they had for her and delighted that, clearly, Gram was the queen bee of this group.

"Young lady, I admire your style."

Freddie turned to gaze into the merry eyes of a man who seemed to be as old as the hills. He had exquisite silver hair and a sun-bronzed face.

When she looked perplexed, he explained. "I met you years ago when you were still in high school. Pax brought you by my studio. I'm Storm Bartholomew and I do like your style." He nodded toward the showroom. "I mean your weaving out there in the gallery. I like your grandma, too, but it is great to have a youngster join us.

"Actually, I asked GG to marry me once but she wouldn't have me." He grinned and raised his voice to tease GG. "I'd still marry her – been a widower more than twenty years – but the last time I proposed, she called me an old coot!" His laughter was a jubilant explosion rippling through the room.

Freddie could hear her Gram sputtering as she fought to maintain her own composure. "Mr.

Bartholomew," she began.

"Storm," he corrected. "Call me Storm."

"Storm," Freddie continued, "as handsome as you are, I suspect you have no trouble finding women who appreciate you. Are you still carving? What is your main interest now?"

"Oh, shoot. I'm not sure. Eating, I suspect. And chasing old women." He gave GG an impish, teasing glance. "Appreciate? I just want to find some old gal that won't fight with me all the time. But she has to be able to cook like your grandma."

"Freddie," Elaine interrupted, laughing. "Storm Bartholomew happens to be one of the finest wood carvers in the world. We can't get enough of his work for the gallery."

Storm grinned shyly. "My ma used to weave. Raised her own sheep for wool. I used to have to go out and climb the hills to herd 'em in for shearing."

"I thought they used sheep dogs for that."

"Not in the mountains. Shoot, kid, I *was* the dog." Again his laughter filled the room. More seriously he added, "My ma used to say that her weaving took away the loneliness of an endless day – when the snow was too deep to walk anywhere."

"Yes," Gram said, "In those dark winter days, you could weave your life into something bright and beautiful – blending colors and coming up with new patterns."

People were gathering up their notebooks and carrying their mugs to a small sink. Freddie studied the faces of the assemblage. This vital, happy group surely shattered any stereotype one might have of older people. A number of craftsmen were represented in the room and Freddie felt herself being drawn into their enthusiasm. Each of them projected a genuine pride in fine artistry, and a desire to pass the skill on to others.

Her grandmother had so many wonderful friends and admirers that Freddie felt a twinge of loneliness, acutely aware that Pax was not in his gallery today. As hurt as she was by his actions, she found herself missing him terribly.

"GG, doesn't weaving take a lot of patience?" Mrs. Olson asked. "I never had the patience to weave."

"Wal, Hilda, the patience seemed natural most of the time. Only once – when my granddaughter left – I got to jerking hard on the beater. Got frustrated, gave it a jerk and ruined my weaving."

Freddie looked at her watch and tried to propel Gram toward the door, but Susan intercepted. "I wish you could have been here all afternoon, to help with the planning. You're one of the artists, you know. Pax says you're one of the best."

"One of these artists? Oh, Susan, you are being kind. Would that I had their incredible talent."

"But you do." Susan grinned. "Pax says so, and he's never wrong. By the way, when're you coming over to see our house? It'll be finished soon."

Freddie chose to ignore the reference to Pax. "I do want to come see your house as soon as I can. Maybe tomorrow after work."

They were almost to the door, and Storm was holding it open when Elaine delayed them. "Thank you so much for coming, Freddie. We couldn't get along without your grandmother and . . . I assume you are here to stay?"

"Yes'um she is," Gram declared.

"That a girl!" Storm said, "Keep her here. Now, let me take you two to dinner."

"Storm, don't start that agin. Anyway, Marge has ours ready. I still git awful tired. You come eat with us," she invited, without enthusiasm.

"Next time." He smiled. "Man, are we glad to have you back, kid. I hope you never leave your grandma again. She's swell when everything is going her way, but, wow, she's a sight when she's upset. Can't stand the woman when she gets frustrated!"

"Piffle," Gram said when they were out of earshot. "The old coot's a fool."

Chapter Fifteen

Gram turned from the kitchen window to inspect her granddaughter from head to toe. "Well," she said finally, "you don't look quite so peaked this morning."

"I'm going to be fine, Gram."

" 'Course you are. A girl like you needs love."

"I have love. More than I deserve or can live up to. You have given me love all of my life."

"What do you call what you have given me?"

Freddie smiled. Gram had improved since Freddie's return. Freddie reached over to pat the tiny blue-veined hand that looked as fragile as a dove's egg. "What time does Marge come?"

"Ain't coming today. Gonna start coming in twice a week instead of ever day."

"Gram, you *are* getting better!"

"I'm getting well."

"Listen, dear one, why don't you plan an early dinner with me. I'm going to grab a sandwich right after work and hike over to see Susan's new house – unless you want to go. I can drive."

"Won't be too many more days like this one promises to be. You jest hurry home and take your little hike,"

"I'll miss Dollie. I always do when I go out on foot. Who will chase the snakes away?"

"Land's sake, child, ain't many snakes in this high altitude – least ways, not poisonous ones. You ain't in Arizona."

####

In spite of the dull ache in her heart, Freddie hoped her face would reflect the glory of the fall day. She slipped on a cotton shirt and jeans and stepped into the yard. There had been no cars at Susan's house on her way out from work and she fully expected to be able to poke around and explore by herself. She could hear no sounds of traffic or heavy equipment and power tools.

The skies were clear except one high jet contrail and a few cirrus clouds. It would soon be winter and such hikes would be out of the question. She shivered. Where were her sweaters? Perhaps Gram had given them away. She kept forgetting to ask. She needed to check on their wood supply and hoped to get the house painted and a new roof before winter. She must remember to talk with her grandmother about it.

This afternoon, she was determined to focus on pleasant thoughts. She smiled when her steps startled a small brown chipmunk. She heard the twittering notes of a slate-colored junco, skirting around near her, unafraid.

Breaking off a dried goldenrod and recalling its delicate anise scent in late summer, she took a deep sniff. The wandlike stem swayed with its heavy flower head, making a rustling sound as she waved it; hundreds of tiny yellow disk flowers had long since faded, leaving dried seed pods.

Lots of things had faded or died. She remembered her own words, less than a week before . . .

"The air has never been more crystal clear and sparkling."

Pax chortled. "Air can't sparkle."

"It does today."

"Sparkle? It's crisp and it's clear and it's nippy. But it does not sparkle. You are sparkling."

Freddie bit her lip. How could life take a tumble into a complete hundred eighty degrees so quickly?

She walked briskly until Gram's private driveway turned onto Turkey Hollow Road and continued quietly up the next drive until she had made sure that the building site was deserted. She walked around it and up the narrow wooden plank at the back door that served, temporarily, in place of stairs. The rhythm of her step caused the plank to spring, putting a bounce in her step like one of the dancing puppets grandpa made for her as a child. Stepping quickly off the plank, she inhaled the sweet smell of new wood. No wonder Susan was excited. What it must feel to be building a house with a man you loved and who loved you.

She was standing where she imagined the kitchen window would be, looking up the canyon at the mountains when the caravan drove up. An evening work party and she was trapped inside! She was as self-conscious as a thief.

A truck door slammed and Pax walked up the front door plank. He stopped when he saw her, balancing himself with his arms spread out as the plank swayed.

They gawked at each other and Freddie sputtered, "I thought you were gone on a buying trip."

"I thought you would be in Phoenix by now."

Her heart raced as though she had run all the way from home. He looked feverish. His eyes were dark embers of smoldering pain. She had not expected *him* to be hurting.

"You said . . . " he blurted.

The sounds of slamming car doors and laughing people was disconcerting for a moment but she had eyes only for him and a terrible awareness of the shock and pain in his face.

Susan spied Freddie and came bounding up the plank, causing a bouncing motion that nearly upset Pax. He grabbed the edge of the door casing and stepped into the unfinished house, completely oblivious of Susan's rambunctious entrance.

"You said you would come," Susan gushed. She swirled glibly past Pax, unaware of his dilemma or the blanched color around his eyes and nose.

When Eddie summoned him, Pax was torn between his commitment to help and Freddie – moving forward onto the ball of his foot, and rocking back again onto his heel, see-sawing as he reached toward her. "Don't move! Stay right there. I'll be right back."

Pax's distress reflected her own conflict between pity and contempt. In spite of what she felt, she pointedly ignored him to greet Susan with an exaggerated benevolence.

Susan's face slid into wide-eyed contortion as she opened her mouth, worked her jaws before she gulped. "Say," she asked in a high, squeaky, little-girl voice, "are you two dating again?"

"Does it look like it?" Freddie muttered.

Susan edged backwards and continued to stare at her. "Sounds like a lover's quarrel to me."

Freddie groaned. She was not especially amiable when she asked, "Is this your kitchen?"

The next thirty minutes might have been comic, had Freddie watched it from outside herself.

"Stay right there," Pax had yelled as he began backing his descent down the plank at the front door. "I just need to help unload." Eddie caught his arm and steadied him as he turned around.

She did not see him walk into a two by six being carried into the building. When he whirled around with a large sheet of plywood across his shoulders, Eddie had to duck to avoid being decapitated. He tripped over a fifty-pound box of nails. All the men were watching Pax worriedly.

It took an unbelievable amount of effort to keep her mind on the details Susan was expounding. "The love seat will fit here, the couch here. We'll use the smaller bedroom as an office until we need it for a nursery."

As soon as she felt it was polite to do so, Freddie congratulated Susan on the house and tried to escape.

"But Pax said to wait here," Susan said.

"I don't work for Pax," she responded ungraciously. "And you are not my keeper," she added when she saw Susan making a valiant effort to signal him. "I don't want a scene, so I am leaving quietly – the way I came."

Freddie had not walked far, however, when Pax's truck pulled up along side her. She fanned the air. "You're stirring up dust."

He leaned out the window. "Get in and I'll take you home."

"I'm walking." She gritted her teeth.

"We need to talk."

"We did." Swinging her arms, she continued her journey.

"Fred, please!" He sounded desperate. "I thought you were leaving. You said you were going to call about the job."

"I did," she retorted, eyes straight ahead, arms slashing the air.

"Well, didn't you?"

"Did I say it or did I – what are you asking?"

"Are you going to talk with me?"

"I am talking with you." She marched on.

He shoved the Bullet into gear, throwing gravel from spinning tires, and shot ahead, fishtailing. She paid attention then, but when he stopped and jumped out of the cab, she almost spooked. He came back to walk beside her. Extending his arms toward her in a plea, he asked. "Why are you angry with me? You're the one who called Phoenix."

The game was getting wearisome. Finally, she stopped and faced him. "Do you remember me telling you that Gram was afraid I would leave again?"

"You were terribly upset."

"Pax. I bared my soul to you. I told you I would never leave here again. You comforted me, kissed away my tears, but – you didn't believe me."

She could have struck him smack across the face with a two by four, with much less pain to him. He recoiled. "But you called your friend, all excited to take the job!" His voice had raised a full octave; his eyes were clouded with uncertainty.

"I called Jill to tell her to apply for the job.

Why would I want a job in Phoenix? Or child care?"

Wearily, he replied, "I wondered if you were keeping something from me."

She stepped gingerly around him and continued her walk, but more slowly now.

He caught up with her, stepped directly in front of her, blocking her escape, and placed a hand on each shoulder. She ducked and wriggled around him. He caught her and scooped her up off the ground and placed her on the truck's hood.

"Listen to me! I am the worst kind of a jerk. I guess we have both been through our own private hells!" He forced her to look at him with a gentle hand on each side of her face. "Darling, I thought seriously about locking you up to keep you from going, but I knew I couldn't keep you against your will. I was devastated when I thought you were leaving again. I've done you a horrible injustice, and I'm sorry."

She was crying hard now. He pulled her head against his chest, and she could feel his labored breathing.

"My precious sweetheart," he whispered. They clutched each other for a long time, and then his voice was a soft whisper. "I could spend the rest of my life doing penitence and it would not be enough. You can never know how sorry I am. We have lost so much time. We need to move on."

"I'm not sure I can." She sniffled.

"Trouble with you, Fred, you don't believe in yourself." He pushed her back from him to look into her eyes. His voice was gruff, and he spoke intensely now. "You don't like yourself, much less anyone else."

She wiped her eyes. "If you fouled up your life like I have, would you like yourself?"

"You *life?* Your *life* is messed up? Come on, Fred." As he warmed to his subject, he threw his arms into the air, nearly dislodging her. "Life? I think my life began that night when you stepped off the bus in Morganton."

Her mouth fell open and she gaped at him speechlessly.

He gathered her into his arms and continued. "I never heard the likes of such tommy-rot in my whole life. Life? I see us building a house together." He gestured broadly with his right arm. "I see raising our kids together, and grandchildren, too. I see us growing old together. Don't you dare speak of life in the past tense!"

"But – but – "

He took her face in his hands, and she trembled because of the love in his eyes. "Do you actually believe that four measly years could destroy my love for you? I'll love you a lifetime."

She closed her eyes and leaned toward his lips, and she thought her heart would burst with joy. Around them she could hear the soft evening cooings of birds and the gentle rustling sounds of forest animals settling down for the night. Mother Nature provided fireworks, hurling flames of pink and orange across the sky behind them.

She perched on the hood of his truck, caressing the shoulders of the big man, nibbling at his ear and they both whispered declarations of love and commitment.

Much later, she tucked a happy grandmother into bed and climbed the stairs to her own room. Her heart sang. She had no fear of nightmares.

But in the blackest part of the night:

She tried to scream, but a searing pain burned her chest. Terrified, she continued to run. The awful fear clawed at her throat like a wild thing.

It was hard to maintain her balance and stay upright: the black mud was deep and the exhaustion staggering. Brad was closing in – grappling, tearing at her clothes.

The other man was running beside her now, big as a mountain. Unsmiling, he extended his hand. She clutched it and its warmth charged through her and became her lifeline. She continued to cling to his hand as their feet gained better traction, and the mire could not thwart their escape. Racing together, they ran swiftly. The fatigue became more endurable as they far outdistanced the violent man who had once threatened her life.

She woke up, but the darkness held no terror. She lay, wrapped in peace and she whispered, "I am really, finally, home at last."

Chapter Sixteen

Anyone who knew Susan could tell when she was more exited than usual. The dinner Gram and Marge fixed to welcome their new neighbors was definitely one of those times.

Periodically, she would wrap her arms across her chest and around her shoulders and squeeze herself, at the same time uttering a series of little bird-like squeaks. Always vivacious, her energy must have been measured out with a heavy hand. Freddie watched her out of the corner of her eyes with a growing concern.

Three times during the course of the meal, Susan leaned across the table and asked Pax, "When are you going to tell them?"

Three times Eddie tried to calm her, finally exclaiming in exasperation, "You're jumpy as a cat in a room full of rocking chairs! What's with you tonight?"

Freddie wondered if Pax was teasing Susan, but there was a gleam in his eyes also. "GG has gone to a lot of work tonight, Susan. I don't want to throw a monkey wrench into her evening."

"What's going on?" Freddie asked when she could stand the suspense no longer.

Finally, Pax laid aside his dessert fork and pulled his coffee cup closer. No one listening to his quiet voice and hearing his explanation would have ever dreamed of the serious repercussions of his announcement. "GG, your weaving has caused quite a stir in Asheville, and beyond. Some big name reporter – er – ah – "

"Ms. Kim Rosser-Gibson," Susan supplied.

"Thanks, Susan. A reporter name Kim Rosser-Gibson is coming to this county to do a series of stories on mountain crafts and artists – "

" – and our gallery."

Pax shook his head and rolled his eyes. "My boy – Eddie," he intoned,"you have your work cut out for you. Yes, she will spend one day at the gallery and wants to spend one day with you, GG. And she's bringing her cameraman."

GG looked dumbfounded. "Me? How come? Land's sake."

"Because you're the best!" Susan blurted, unable to contain herself. Eddie gazed at her adoringly, in spite of Pax's dire prediction.

"The Mountain Heritage Museum recommended that she come interview you," Pax explained. "I've been trying to build up some press for some time. I met her a few weeks ago when I was on a buying trip. She'll also interview a few others, like Storm."

"But I ain't working now."

"Yes, you are. I've seen some of your new designs. But even if you were not working right now, she'd be interested in the whole of your work."

"I don't want no woman reporter, especially one with a double hinged name like that, to come poke around my place."

"Why, GG? Are you afraid of her?" Eddie asked and winked at Freddie. "You could become a celebrity. Maybe famous, and even rich!"

"'Course I ain't scared of her." Gram was indignant. "But, I'll throw a camera smack outta here. Too many wrinkles. Look like a washboard."

Susan sounded appalled. "Why, GG, I never knew you had a vain cell in your body. You are a beautiful woman."

"Ha! Maybe for a hundred-twenty-year-old."

"Gram, you certainly wouldn't want Storm to get all the publicity. This reporter might be a pretty girl who would take a shine to Storm."

"Piffle. That old – "

"Gram," her granddaughter warned.

Pax grinned at Freddie. "Fred will be here on Saturday and she can demonstrate the weaving, if you don't want to. It can mean a lot to the mountain craftsmen, GG. It will give us some good promotion for the fair, also. "

"Wal, all right," she agreed begrudgingly. "Only don't expect me to smile for no camera."

Susan stared at the ceiling. "I've been thinking. I can use Deerfoot-Miller as my married name."

Eddie choked on his coffee.

Pax invited Freddie to come to the gallery Friday morning to meet Ms. Kim Rosser-Gibson, but she declined with an amused smile. She had the distinct opinion that he would rather do anything, possibly undergo a root canal, than to submit to the reporter's questions and camera. He was a shy man by nature and tried to arrange a last minute out-of-state buying trip, but his partner threatened mutiny.

Elaine and Susan were both basking in the unaccustomed limelight and the commotion it entailed. Freddie, Bettie Lou and Don accomplished only a trifling amount of work at the plumbing supply because of the necessity of staring out the window and across the highway to watch the excitement.

First, a florist truck arrived and several large bouquets were carried into the gallery. Even so, Susan hurried breathlessly across the highway to borrow an arrangement from Bettie Lou. "We forgot the ladies' room," she explained.

Ms. Kim Rosser-Gibson arrived just after nine in a sunshine yellow MGB convertible. She wore a matching yellow business suit. She was tall and glamorous and her hair shone like black jet. Freddie wondered how she was able to fold compactly enough to fit into the toylike car – or how she was able to drive wearing spike heels.

A long silver van with *Regional Headline Journal* emblazoned in red and black on the side slid into the parking lot. Three men, presumably photographers, unloaded a truckload of cameras, tripods and lights. Shortly after their gear was hauled into the gallery, a delivery turned up from *Daily Delights Donuts*.

Ms. Kim Rosser-Gibson had just begun her tour when the local press arrived to cover *her* coverage of Palmer Gallery.

Pax was fit to be tied about the last complication, according to Susan when she rushed back to Bittle Plumbing to call in a report to her fiancé. "He doesn't know who called the local reporters," she said in a conspiratorial tone.

"But I can guess. Ms. Hoity-Toity is in the habit of her own entourage from the press corps. She's playing the lofty big time investigative reporter to the hilt. She even has a video camera in there in case she can get a spot on Atlanta television!" She rolled her eyes, then dropped her voice. "She acts like she has something on Pax. There's something sinister and scary going on."

Freddie laughed to herself. Susan could be ludicrous when she became dramatic and let her imagination shift into overdrive.

Rumors filtered back to Bittle Plumbing, via customers and friends who dropped by. Mrs. Olson was entranced by all the excitement. "Why Ms. Rosser-Gibson acts like a reporter from *PrimeTime.* She is going to buy some of my candles. But, you know what? She flirts outrageously with Mr. Palmer. She is also kinda haughty, but then, I guess she *is* a big shot and we *are* just country people."

The real fun commenced with an afternoon mountain thunderstorm. Ms. Rosser-Gibson had failed to secure her convertible roof in the dazzling morning sunlight and the foreign sports car nearly washed away before someone recognized the situation. It appeared that no one else knew how to raise the vinyl top and a local photographer had to hold the golf umbrella above her head as she negotiated the flooded parking lot in high heels. She pointed to the tonneau cover located behind the seat and waited for a coterie of press personnel to hoist up the roof in the rain.

Considering everything Freddie was a little apprehensive about the Saturday interview scheduled with her grandmother. Gram would not tolerate a snob.

Weave Me a Song

Chapter Seventeen

It turned out to be one of the strangest days in Freddie's life.

Early, long before the reporter was to appear on the scene, Gram became alarmed by a suspicious-looking man prowling around the property. Freddie could see no car, but as he strolled closer, she saw a camera bag slung across his shoulder. "I think it's a cameraman who works with Ms. Rosser-Gibson. He must be parked out on Turkey Hollow Road."

"He ain't got no right–"

"He won't hurt anything."

"Could of asked," Gram snorted.

The cameraman was not the same one who came to the house with Ms. Rosser-Gibson. Freddie noticed that she did not come in her cute little yellow car. It was still possibly dripping rainwater.

A long delay followed the arrival of a gray sedan, with *RHJ* painted on the door. They had heard doors slam when the couple got out of the car, but when Freddie looked through the window, Ms.

Rosser-Gibson was standing near the porch, obviously agitated. Freddie opened the door, puzzled. The reporter merely pointed, aghast. On the porch railing a bushy tailed squirrel chomped serenely on an acorn.

Gram leaned on her cane and stared. "Woman, that's jest Dan'l Boone. Been our pet for years. He won't bite you." She tapped the floor with her cane and the animal shot off the porch. "Lessen you try to grab him, a course."

Cautiously, Ms. Rosser-Gibson placed her foot on the step as daintily as though she were wearing glass slippers, and pulled herself up along the railing.

"You scared of a squirrel?" Gram chuckled delightedly.

"In the city we have been cautioned that they carry rabies." She was dressed in a fashionable, but very short, black suit. The solitary note of color was a brilliant red scarf draped around her neck and cascading down the back of her shoulders. Contrasted against the red, her hair was ebony black and her eyes the greenest green eyes Freddie had ever seen. She wore sheer black hose and Freddie marveled that she could walk in four-inch heels.

With a formality that seemed bizarre in Gram's house, she presented an engraved business card and held out her hand. "I am Kim Rosser-Gibson." Her voice was low and smooth as home-churned butter.

Gram looked befuddled. She hesitated and then swiped at the side of her dress as though she felt she had to dust her hand before extending it to this remarkable visitor.

Nodding her head in the general direction of

a young man now climbing the stairs, the reporter acknowledged, "That's Red, my camerman."

Grinning, he pointed to his flaming chestnut hair, explaining his nickname.

Gram said, "Are you a Rosser-Gibson also?"

"Of course not," the reporter snapped. "He's an assistant."

"Red Whitten. Pleased to meet you," he said, extending his hand and ignoring his person-to-be-assisted.

Freddie offered seats but Ms. Rosser-Gibson pointedly ignored her.

Their visitor's eyes darted around the room and settled uncertainly on the fireplace. She chose a straight-backed chair and settled as far away from the fireplace as she could manage. "Could there be other – animals – in here?" she asked.

"Prob'bly," Gram said with a straight face.

"Gram! You know better than that!"

Ms. Rosser-Gibson was momentarily disconcerted, but she recovered quickly. She slid a huge bag off her shoulder and opened it. She clicked on a small, hand-sized tape recorder and placed it on the floor at her feet. She flipped open a notebook and poised her gold pen above it. "Now," she began, "I'll call you Grandma."

"Can't you spell Gouge?"

Ms. Rosser-Gibson looked startled. "If you prefer it – "

"My *pro-fess-i-nol* name is Grandmother Gouge, or GG. You kin call me either of those, or Mrs. Gouge if you like," she added graciously.

The reporter sighed and wrote in her notebook. "Red," she said, ignoring Freddie again, "you might be able to drum up a cup of coffee or something for yourself. Get some outside shots." She waved her hand in the direction of the kitchen.

"Would you like to come with me, Mr. Whitten? I think we can 'drum up' a cup of coffee."

"Red."

"Red. I'm GG's granddaughter, Freddie." They left Ms. Kim Rosser-Gibson at the mercy of her hostess.

####

She poured Red a cup of coffee and warmed him one of Gram's breakfast biscuits. Then he dumbfounded her.

"I hope you don't mind, or snitch on me, if I ask to do something completely unprofessional and dastardly wicked."

Freddie stared at him.

"I think Miss High-and-Mighty has met her match. Would you care if I cracked this door and listened?"

"Red, I like you very much. So, I warn you, this could be brutal."

Grinning, he gingerly slid open the door a half inch and leaned toward the living room.

They heard a voice, with no smile in it, ask curtly, "May I ask how old you are, Grandmother Gouge?"

"May I ask how old *you* are?"

Red's mouth fell open and his eyes opened double their normal size.

Ms. Rosser-Gibson sputtered. "Really, Mrs. Gouge, that's a routine question, quite legitimate."

"So why didn't you answer? 'Cause it's rude, that's why, but anyone as young as you are ought not be ashamed of her age no matter how she looks."

Red covered his mouth with both hands.

"It is a factual statistic that my editor requires. Never mind, I'll ask – "

"Pax don't know."

"Well, I – "

"Jest tell that high-falutin editor that the old woman was born after the turn of the century – the twentieth century."

Red had to close the door. He doubled over, trying desperately to muffle his laugher. His cheeks were bloated and red. He pointed to the back door, and fled.

On the back porch he slumped to the steps and howled with laughter. "I love this country," he said when he was able to talk again. "It's my first trip to the mountains. I love the people I've met. I'm plum crazy about your Gram. And that Storm Bartholomew is no slob either. I nearly died when Kim asked him what the hillbillies up here do in the winter."

"What did Storm say?"

"'We go to Florida to teach school.' How he knew Kim was from Florida, I'll never know." Red cackled with laughter and slapped his leg in mirth. "I wish I could talk my girlfriend into considering this area when we're married. Does your grandmother have any land to sell?"

Freddie was uneasy about getting too far from the house, but Red seemed to assume they had been dismissed for awhile. He wanted to take pictures of Gram's house and the surrounding mountains. He pulled a portable tripod out of his backpack and set it up.

"Do you have any idea why Ms. Rosser-Gibson acts the way she does?"

"Ambition. She's trying to win a Pulitzer. Bitter, vitriolic."

Remembering Susan's comments, she asked, "What does she have against Pax?"

"Probably the fact that he's a good-looking man who didn't take a tumble for her."

"That's reassuring," she said and blushed.

Red turned to grin at her. "Ho, ho, ho! I thought there might be more than just business interest." Then, he grew serious and said, "I have no right to laugh at her. I'm sure a failed marriage is hard enough to get through, but she's eaten up with hatred and has set out to destroy anyone she suspects of being happy. I guess she *has* been through hell. Her ex-husband recently committed suicide. I understand that his publishing business was failing. Kim about went crazy."

It was nearly an hour before Ms. Rosser-Gibson called them back for some publicity shots inside. She seemed about finished with her interview but she also appeared frustrated. "We saw your weaving at the museum in Asheville, Mrs. Gouge. Nice. Tell me about the little weaving you have on display at Palmer Gallery now. We took pictures of it."

"You mean the 'little weaving' on the staircase landing? Wal, that one ain't mine. Done by my granddaughter. When Pax sold my last weaving, he hung that one. Seems to me that if you took pictures, you would've noticed Freddie was the artist. Was it raining or cloudy or something so you couldn't see the signature?"

Ms. Rosser-Gibson ignored the last remark and tried another approach. "Does it bother you that you have not made a lot of money with your craft?"

"How do you know I haven't?"

The reporter was flustered. "Well, I assumed," she said, glancing around the small house. "Paxton Palmer seems to have done quite well."

Gram bristled. "Woman, I sure hope so. He's put his life into helping mountain artists."

"What is the most you have made on a piece of your artwork?"

"More than I care to brag about."

Ms. Rosser-Gibson was bristling now. "Get some pictures of the loom," she snapped at Red. The exasperation crept up her neck as a pink streak that spread across her cheek, almost as though the red scarf was bleeding color. "Make sure you get one that includes the design taped to the top. We'll get Mrs. Gouge up there in a minute. I want her to demonstrate her unique style – the skill that should have made her one of the best paid artists in the Southeast. I trust you got decent shots outside."

Ms. Rosser-Gibson had been sparring with GG all morning. She should have learned her lesson, Freddie thought. Red had said she fancied herself as an "investigative reporter." What was she investigating?

Freddie watched as she crossed her left knee with her elegant right leg and wrapped that leg around her left ankle. She rubbed the back of her stiletto heel up and down the calf of her long limb. She tapped her pen on her cheek as though she were pointing out the location of a toothache. She extended her visual contact to include Freddie in the conversation for the first time. "Several years ago," she began in a conspiratorial tone meant to pull them into her confidence, "I had a close friend in publishing who was working with Mr. Palmer on a book proposal. I believe it contained some of your designs, Mrs. Gouge."

She paused dramatically, measuring their involvement with the book with her pointed disclosure. "Why did he put that on hold? My friend thought he was seeking a high bidder, or, perhaps was waiting until you – well, until you were no longer in the picture."

Freddie's veins filled with ice. She tried to swallow, but her throat felt raw. The room was suddenly oppressive, as though all the oxygen had been sucked out. She could not have responded had her life depended upon it.

Gram had no such reservations. "Wal, Ms. Big Time Reporter, why don't you jest ask Pax? We speak honestly and fairly in these mountains."

Ms. Rosser-Gibson didn't bat an eye, but she smiled condescendingly. "I heard there had been some serious contention between you over it."

"Ain't no contention between us." She laughed. "No fussing, neither. Not hardly. We are planning – well, that would be my granddaughter's business if she wanted to share it with you. But, then, I doubt she will. If you're wanting a picture of me, best get it. I kinda like your assistant, but I am plum tired of your questions. Red, where do you want me to sit?"

Red spun into action and Ms. Rosser-Gibson stood up so quickly that she knocked over her recorder. She walked to the door. She was chewing her lip when Freddie cornered her.

"I don't think I understand your intentions and I wonder where you were trying to go with your interview. Exploitation, I suspect."

"It is called 'professional technique.'" Ms.

Rosser-Gibson's eyes narrowed.

"It is called 'trying to take advantage of an old woman.' I'll see that Mr. Palmer hears about it."

"Oh, now, don't make a mountain out of a molehill. I was trying to help you." Her voice sounded quite weary, suddenly. "Red, make sure you get several good shots of this young lady."

"I think he has all the pictures you'll need. Red, thank you for coming."

Freddie had terminated the interview.

Weave Me a Song

Chapter Eighteen

Freddie grabbed the phone on the first ring, praying it had not disturbed Gram.

"How did GG fare?" Pax asked.

"I think it would be more to the point to ask how Ms. Rosser-Gibson fared!"

A lusty laughter rumbled from the telephone. "That bad, eh? I want to hear all about it. She came back by the gallery, picked up her equipment and shot out of here."

"I would say good riddance. But it wasn't easy on Gram, either. Pax?"

"Is something worrying you, honey? Couldn't have been that bad."

"I think she's a wicked, conniving woman with something up her sleeve that gives me a foreboding of something bad."

Pax chuckled. "You've been talking with Susan, right?"

"You can laugh if you want to, but I'm scared. I thought Susan was being terribly overdramatic yesterday, too. Pax, I actually got so upset that I asked your illustrious reporter to leave. I hated to because I was developing quite a crush on her photographer."

"Was it that awful?"

"I don't know what's wrong, but something is. Something terribly wrong."

"I'll be out just as soon as we close up. And, Fred, leave that red-headed photographer alone."

# # # #

Every minute – every second – of her day was lived in anticipation of the time she had with Pax. She cheerfully filled her days with work and the task of finishing Gram's weaving, but her whole being was attuned to the sound of his steps or the lilt in his voice. As their love grew, she saw all the adoration and affection she bestowed on him reflected back in his eyes.

"Honey," he explained. "This is not the right time to be trying to win a girl. Every cent I could borrow is invested in the gallery. This year will be the making or breaking of our business. Please don't think I'm willingly neglecting you."

"I know, darling. I have grown up a little in the last few years."

She had a favorite image of him. Sometimes she would slip into the darkening gallery after closing hours. Tiptoeing down the staircase toward his office, she could see him slouched over his big, wide desk absorbed in a contract for an artist, his concentration isolating him from every other concern.

The light from the goose-neck lamp accentuated his fatigue. His tie would be pulled off, his white shirt open at the neck and his sleeves rolled up. She could see the furrow of worry lines stretching across his forehead and crow's feet etched around his eyes.

Then she would whisper his name. The worry lines would smooth out miraculously. The crows feet would be transformed into dancing laugh lines as he looked up and smiled, and it would be as though someone had turned on the sunshine. Her heart would melt, and she would become weak behind the knees. It happened every time.

He spent arduous hours at the gallery and on the road trying to find artists to "discover." Elaine used her flair in salesmanship to entice interior decorators who worked along the plush condominiums springing up around the ski slopes.

Freddie was content. She needed time to spend with her grandmother, and she had no doubt about the place she held in his life. She had begun to take bids on some of the repairs around the house: a new roof job before winter and some painting scheduled for spring. Gram had let the maintenance of the property slide during her absence. Freddie found herself wishing it had been done before the appearance of Ms. Rosser-Gibson.

####

Pax bounded up the back steps. "And so, GG, what did you do to our poor reporter?"

"Nothing."

"Okay. What did she do to you?"

"Nothing." But she smiled. "Pathetic city-slicker. No match for this hillbilly."

He laughed and bent to kiss her weathered cheek.

"Poor little creature: scared of a squirrel."

Pax walked across the room to where Freddie

was icing a cake. She raised her lips to his. "You look like a cute little housewife."

"I can't find anyone to marry me."

"The red-headed photographer didn't – "

She wrinkled her nose at him. "He already has a girlfriend."

"Just hang in there, honey, some big galoot will come along and sweep you off your feet – if you're lucky."

Gram asked, "When did you last eat, Pax? Set yourself down. Hot vegetable soup."

"Wow!" He hesitated not at all and as soon as he was seated, he asked Freddie. "So what did this woman say that bothered you so much?"

"She made me leave during her interview."

"What?" he exploded. "On what basis?"

Freddie brushed her hand across her forehead. Pensively she said, "You know, I'm not sure. She didn't look at me. She asked Red to find himself a cup of coffee and just indicated me with a sweep of her hand. Should I have left?"

Pax chuckled. "I think GG was perfectly capable of taking care of herself. What kind of questions did she ask?" He turned to GG.

"Wal, I'll tell you. Land's sake, she mainly wanted to tell me how poor I was. She wanted to know how I had learned to weave and wanted me to say my loom kept my family from starving."

Pax laid down his spoon. He stared at the old lady, his eyes bright and full of admiration.

Gram continued. "She asked all them usual questions. How'd I learn? Who taught me? Did I raise my own sheep? Spin? You know, all them things." She spoke with the aplomb of a seasoned media personality.

"I tried to tell the woman about weaving. Told her I wanted to make something splendid. Told her I wanted to do something worthwhile with my hands. She said, 'But, Mrs. Gouge, the crafts were developed because of extreme poverty.'" Gram pressed her lips together, twisted her shoulder this way and that way, impatiently, doing an apt caricature of Ms. Rosser-Gibson.

"I decided I'd best educate the flatlander. 'Young lady,' I sed, the people in these hills didn't have much cash, but we ate well. We raised food and we made clothes because it was miles to the store. As the years went by, we found out we could make something comely out of homespun yarn and flour sacks.'" Gram paused to take a deep breath.

"She didn't hear a thing I sed. She looked surprised and allowed that there was still poverty up here in these hills."

"I sed," she continued, "'Maybe for some. But I don't weave in order to eat. I reckon I can just sing with my fingers, when I don't know other way. For me it's 'cause I need to express what's inside."

"What did she say to that?" Pax wanted to know, fascinated.

"She took that ridiculous shoe and shoved that little black box closer to me. 'And inside?' she asks. 'Anger at being poor or lonely?' I leaned toward that box and spoke right up. Sed, 'God is love and He cares fer them that loves Him.'"

Pax sighed. "Whew!"

"And?" Freddie's eyes were swimming. She adored her grandmother.

"She looked plum startled. So I tried to tell her about Del and my son and my granddaughter, and weaving and how everything gets all mixed up together when you are a lovin . . . "

"And?" Another prompt because Gram was staring off into space.

"Wish you could 'uv known my Del, Pax. Good man. Gentle man. He'd pull up a chair to watch me weave. 'Weave me a song, Garnet,' he would say. 'I love to watch it grow.'"

There was another long pause as GG remembered. "Gram," Freddie broke into her reverie gently. "What did Ms. Rosser-Gibson say?"

"Didn't say nary a word to me. She stood up quickly and stomped to the door and bellowed out fer her assistant."

For a moment, no one said anything. Then, Pax stood up and walked around the table. He kissed Gram on the forehead. "My darling GG, you are magnificent."

"But wait, Pax. That's not what upset me."

"There's more?" he asked, refilling their coffee cups and sitting back down.

Freddie told him about the "close friend" in publishing, and the book proposal. She could not meet his eyes as she quoted Ms. Rosser-Gibson. "My friend thought that Mr. Palmer was waiting until Mrs. Gouge was no longer in the picture."

Pax leaped to his feet. "That witch! Who was her friend?"

"She didn't say."

Pax walked to the window and stared at the mountains. "Carl something or other. Let me think." He made a fist and pounded it against his forehead. "Carl Gibson! My God. That was his name."

"Her ex-husband," Freddie said dully. "Her ex-husband, who recently committed suicide. Red told me about it."

Pax came back to the table. He pulled his chair directly in front of GG, sat down and took her hands in his. "It wasn't like that," he said earnestly, and continued his explanation in spite of the finger she raised to his lips to hush him.

"I dropped the proposal for three reasons. I didn't like Gibson; couldn't trust him. He was supposed to return the proposal, but he never did. The originals disappeared. I never saw the paperwork or the designs again after you left, Fred." He turned to look at her. "I just lost all interest in the project. Perhaps I was unfair to GG, but I couldn't go on. Then, I forgot all about it when I got involved with the renovations."

Freddie had turned pale. "You thought I had taken the designs?"

"Either you, or *him*."

"Oh, Pax." Her eyes were full of pain. She whispered, "You must have despised me. Now, *that woman* means to destroy you to avenge her husband's death."

GG shook her head, sadly. "Revenge is a tragic thing."

"How can she hurt me? Let her try. Are you going to cut that cake?" he asked and GG issued a delighted little grunt of pleasure.

A few minutes later, between bites he said, "I wonder . . . "

They both waited for him to explain.

"Mrs. Olson came by this afternoon and gathered up every one of her candles and took them away. I kept her work on consignment merely to help her. I certainly don't make any profit on her work. She was vague and defensive. Do you suppose Rosser-Gibson got to her? And if she got to her, how many other artists did she talk with? We know she tried you."

A premonition of danger swept through Freddie. She looked so worried that Pax put his arm around her and pulled her to his shoulder.

"Piffle!" Gram said. "She can't hurt you."

Chapter Nineteen

Late one evening a copy of the *Regional Headline Journal* was delivered by special messenger to Pax at the gallery. He opened the paper and spread it across his desk.

Terrific photographs accompanied Kim Rosser-Gibson's article. Pax was pleased. He was going to have a good laugh on Fred and Susan. Pictures presented the elegant facade of the gallery and there was an excellent coverage of displays he had designed and built himself. A prominent photograph featured Storm Bartholomew demonstrating one of his coveted marionettes. Pax smiled. He began to read.

"From a parking lot that includes several sleek, powerful automobiles, Paxton Palmer habitually selects a ragged pickup, with a lot of body rust from road salt, to use on his buying trips into the backwoods. He chooses the older vehicle to ingratiate himself with the mountain people from whom he secures top-notch art for his prestigious gallery. Thanks to the work of local people, Palmer Gallery of Ash Hill, North Carolina, only twelve miles from the Blue Ridge Parkway, has made a successful man out of its owner."

Pax was perplexed. The Bullet was his only transportation. "Palmer Gallery has gained a reputation of preeminence," Ms. Rosser-Gibson wrote, "although its artists live much as they have for years, on the verge of poverty, in spite of gaining homage in the arts and crafts world. Palmer has done extensive, costly renovations, producing one of the most elite galleries on the East Coast, and he still manages to command respect from many art collectors."

Pax paused. What on earth did she mean by that? Frowning, he studied the other photographs. There was a wide shot of Gram's house, nestled in between towering ridges. The photograph caught a glimpse of the old chicken coop and barn and gave the impression that all the buildings were on the verge of collapsing. The closeup was a vivid portrayal of GG sitting at her loom.

"Grandma Gouge, the prize winning star that made Palmer Gallery famous, is no longer selling her work there," the article continued. Pax's mouth fell open. "The display that used to feature her exquisite wall hangings now plays up the apprentice-quality weaving of her attractive granddaughter, Frederica Gouge. *Headline Journal* had to travel to Mountain Heritage Museum in Asheville to see Grandma Gouge's work."

He read on, his insides churning. "Some of Palmer's exhibitors wonder if they are being exploited. One skilled candlemaker told this reporter that she is no longer able to eke out a living selling to this gallery. A leading community businessman suggested that Palmer is getting rich off the backs of the Appalachian poor."

Pax' first reaction was one of stunned disbelief. Then, he grew furious – as fighting mad as he had ever been in his life. He was shaking all over. His breathing grew shallow; his throat felt fur-lined and his stomach clenched like a fist. How dared she! The unfairness of the article made him sick. He wanted to howl out his anguish, but he hardly had the strength to pick up a phone to call his partner Elaine – or Fred.

He balled up the paper and slammed it across the room. He sat very still for a long time. He needed to call Elaine. They may have delivered the scurrilous rag to her.

What he wanted to do was to go to Fred. But he could not share this trash with her. Not tonight. Not yet.

The phone jarred him. He could not remember ever jumping at the sound of the telephone's ringing before.

"Pax?"

He could tell by Elaine's voice that she had also received the poisonous paper.

"Are you alone?" he asked and was relieved to know that her husband was with her. "Try not to worry. Not many people around here are familiar with that smear sheet."

"But Pax – oh, I can't talk. Let Lamar tell you."

Her husband took the phone. "I'd like to strangle one stinking reporter. I never heard of such asinine toxicity!"

"Tell Elaine, and you believe it, too, that we'll weather this storm." He wished he felt the confidence he tried to project.

"But that virulent witch sent Elaine a note saying a copy of the venom was going to each interior decorator that she works with."

Pax sank wearily into his chair. "The woman is depraved. But, hold on, Lamar, someone's banging on the door. I'll call you back."

Lamar yelled into the phone. "Don't open the door! You may be in danger. I'm coming over."

Whoever was assailing the place was about to cave the door in. They were attacking with a vengeance. Pax snapped back the dead bolt and yanked the door open. Storm Bartholomew nearly fell across the sill.

"What the devil!" he was yelling, and shaking a paper at him. "Explain this, if you please." His face was red and the veins in his neck looked like they were about to pop.

"Storm, calm down. I can't explain it." He felt as though his knees were going to buckle.

"You *are* going to sue the bitch, aren't you? Never heard such foul drivel in all my years put together. You got a lawyer – or shall I call mine?"

Pax stepped forward and smothered his startled visitor with a bear hug. "Great Scott, Storm! You scared me to death. I thought you were going to tear me apart."

Storm shoved him back to glare at him. Pax had never heard him swear before but firecrackers could not have lit up the gallery more. "Don't insult me, man. Aren't we friends? That yellow striped she-skunk!"

For the first time all evening, Pax relaxed. He was laughing when Lamar Saunders came tearing into the gallery, wild-eyed, clearly expecting mayhem. Lamar was gasping as he spotted Storm. He gave a sigh of relief. "I thought you were being ambushed," he said, still puffing. His chest heaved with each breath

"I was." Pax grinned. "Thanks for coming."

"You a lawyer?" Storm demanded.

"I'm afraid not. I'm a history professor."

"I knew you were one of those *in-tel-lect-uals.* You ever hear of such foul drivel?"

"I can't say I have. Abominable. What's she got to gain by this?"

Storm was pacing the floor. "I say we hire a good lawyer and sue."

Pax laid a hand on the older man's shoulder. "No, wait, Storm. We can't rush into this. Did she say anything actually libelous? Unnamed sources. I hate that cop-out."

"Lies. All of them lies." The little man paced back and forth.

"Yes," Lamar said, "but cleverly worded. What she wrote is not the biggest problem; it's what she does with the garbage that's what we have to worry about."

"Perhaps we're rushing to judgement. Could be that no one will pay any attention to her." He prayed he was right.

Lamar shook his head. "She's mailing tear sheets to all your clients and customers. I'd better call Elaine or she'll have an ambulance and the sheriff over here."

"And I have to call Fred." He sat down and a gloom, so dense he could have fanned it like heavy smoke, settled over his office.

####

Pax felt as though he was trying to climb out a deep, dark well. A dull heaviness, like an iron weight, never left his gut. The unfairness and injustice of the whole situation kept him sick.

The first indication of serious trouble came from a source that would have been insignificant in less tense days. One by one sponsors of the craft fair called to cancel. Those sponsors represented the community and Pax was deeply disturbed. One of the most humiliating aspects of the tragedy was that it was so public.

The telephone calls were next, anonymous calls spewing putrid hate messages and violent threats about burning the building.

The trashings should have been no surprise, but they were such villainous actions. The three mornings since the *Regional Headline Journal* appeared, Pax arrived at work to find the parking lot and steps leading to the gallery strewn with garbage. He finally brought his sleeping bag to his office and spent the nights there.

He stood with Elaine and looked out at the empty parking lot. Two interior decorators had cancelled appointments that day alone. "I wish I had the money so I could buy your interest out. I don't want to take you down too."

Elaine protested. "Lamar and I noticed that you didn't try to buy us out the months we made record sales."

One day his pastor came to the gallery. He offered no empty platitudes. There were no sermons, no reprimands. He walked through the gallery and admired the displays. "I want to buy that little birdhouse for my wife for Christmas," he said and it was the first sale of the week.

"Pax," Rev. Kimble said, "when this is over – and it will be over – we'll have lunch together."

Pax felt infinitely better. That night he began calling each of his artists. He offered to release them from their contracts. "I have been as fair as I know how," he explained, "but check around and see if you can find a better deal."

The first two people he called scoffed about any possibility of exploitation. The third man said he would check around to see what kind of commissions the other galleries were charging.

The fourth call sent cold chills down Pax's spine. He recognized the voice of the hate caller.

The task was a grueling undertaking but he spend every evening methodically contracting each person whose work he represented. His confidence was bolstered as he continued. Ninety-nine percent of his clients knew he was honest and fair, but he didn't have a clue as to how to get the message across to his customers.

"We'll weather the storm," he had said but on a late night telephone call to Freddie his voice broke. "Life is not fair, kid."

Weave Me a Song

Chapter Twenty

Freddie started spending her lunch break with Pax, packing a meal for him also. "You look cadaverous, darling," she said, trying to lighten the mood by teasing him. But really, his hollow-eyed and dispirited look had her frightened. "Gram says you need to eat."

"If this continues, we're faced with bankruptcy," he admitted. "I had to lay Susan off and don't know how long we can pay the electric bill. Some of our best art that had been out on approval has been returned, with caustic notes, and sales have been absolutely nil. Our only sale in two weeks has been a birdhouse."

"I have a message from Gram. She said to tell you she hasn't cashed the check on the last weaving and you can borrow that."

Pax shook his head, but he smiled. "Tell her I miss her. If I quit getting the threatening calls – a lunatic's idea of a sadistic joke, I think – I'll stop spending so much time here. But, you know, if we can make it through this, it will be worth it, *almost.* I never dreamed I had so many friends. Out of all the people I called, the only person whose work I returned was one who didn't ask for it back. When I recognized Pike's voice as the hate caller, I simply boxed up his work and left it on his porch."

She put her arms around him. "I've never been so proud of anyone in my life."

His kiss was passionate. "I'll make up all this lost time with you sometime, Fred."

On her way out, she was surprised to see Mrs. Olson browsing around in the gallery. "Have you seen any of my candles?" she asked Freddie. "I can't find them anywhere."

Freddie touched the small woman on the arm. "Don't you remember the reporter from Atlanta? You told her you were not going to sell your candles here anymore."

"Reporter?" She knitted her brows and tilted her head in concentration. "Oh, that one that promised to buy all my candles? She never came to pick them up."

Elaine had been listening, and she stepped closer. "Mrs. Olson, do you have some candles you would like to sell here?"

Mrs. Olson looked puzzled. "Don't I have any here? I can't find them."

Freddie groaned inwardly. Rosser-Gibson had exploited the unfortunate woman, putting words in her mouth and leaving her empty-handed.

Elaine continued talking to the confused woman. "Mrs. Olson, would you be willing to explain that to a friend of mine who works for the local newspaper? Ms. Rosser-Gibson said you told her Mr. Palmer was taking advantage of you."

"Dear, Mr. Palmer would do no such thing."

"Ms. Rosser-Gibson told a lot of people that you said he had. I want to call a friend. Will you talk with her? She might want to take a picture of you for *The Avery Sentinel*."

"How lovely, dear. I *would* like to be holding one of my candles in it, but I can't find them."

"You come into the office. I'll call my friend and we can go get some of your candles."

####

The cloudy, dark day matched Freddie's melancholy. It seemed to her that it had been raining for days. She worried about the river, but she dismissed the possibility of a flooding danger, opened her umbrella and walked back across the highway to Bittle Plumbing.

She supposed it would be another evening without Pax. She knew his life's work was invested in the gallery, and also that it represented the livelihood of many others, but she was lonely. What was it Red had told her about Rosser-Gibson? She no longer thought of her in terms of Kim Rosser-Gibson or even Ms. In Freddie's mind she had lost any resemblance to a human personality.

Red had said, "She's eaten up with hatred and has set out to destroy anyone she suspects having great happiness."

She certainly could not "destroy" them, but she was doing a good job of making their lives miserable. What could she possibly gain by doing it?

All night the storm continued to build. A relentless rain and wind as fierce as a wolverine blasted down the mountains. It sliced power and telephone lines and stripped all remaining leaves, leaving somber-looking gray skeletons of trees in its wake. Freddie was uneasy about leaving her grandmother alone and driving into town.

"Don't be silly," Gram said. "I have lived through all sorts of storms and floods and the worst kind of blizzards. Anyway, Marge can check on me."

"But if the power's out, I won't be able to work anyway."

Gram shook her head. "Go, child. I'm fearful for Pax this morning. You need to be close to him."

Usually, she loved the high country in early winter when the evergreens blended with the gray hardwoods, presenting a silver-dappled landscape, giving the mountains a patina, like priceless antique metal. It signaled the end of summer tourists and began the lull before the winter tourist season, giving the year-rounders the mountains to themselves for a few short weeks.

The wind whipped her umbrella and she was drenched before she could get to her car. She felt a strange, frightening sense of doom. Some roads were already flooded, others closed off by downed trees. The closer she got to Bittle Plumbing, the darker the sky became. The sounds of huge raindrops pelting the windshield nearly drowned out the radio but she heard the evacuation warning for several communities near Foscoe. The wind made it difficult to keep the car on the road.

Along the river she saw trucks from the Emergency Management Crew and volunteers filling sandbags, the rain nearly obscuring their images. Occasionally she met emergency vehicles: ambulances and fire trucks. She had to pull over onto the muddy shoulder, hoping to God her car would not get stuck. Other than that, the highway seemed practically deserted.

The Linville River, which usually sang and danced its way to the Atlantic, had turned into a raging, turbulent dragon, spewing foam and fury, threatening to devour everything in its path. It was biting at cabins perched along its banks and gobbling at the bridges that dared to cross it.

She pulled as close to Bittle Plumbing as she could manage and staggered into the building in the drenching downpour. She made a beeline for the front window, ignoring her dripping clothes. Pax had moved his truck uphill. It stood isolated in the parking lot, spotlighted by lightning like a lone sentinel on some endangered outpost.

"Are the phones working?" she asked.

"Yes, but to be used only for emergencies. Pax couldn't hear it, anyway. He's down below the office area," Bettie Lou explained. "We saw him take his shovel out a minute ago."

Don came up behind her. "I suspect he thinks drowning is the least of his troubles?"

"I'm going over there."

"Brilliant. Add to his worries?"

The water rose in the gallery parking lot. In occasional flashes of lightning, it looked as shiny as a piece of plate glass. Fear choked Freddie.

Don continued to talk. "He's gonna lose it. He can't save his gallery without help? Lots of help?"

Tears streamed down her face. "How much more heartache can the man take? What can we do? Don, we have to do something! Maybe he could evacuate the lower levels. He has expensive art stored there. We need men and trucks – "

Don turned to stare at her. He seemed disappointed in her. He shook his head in disbelief.

"Lady, you have been away too long."

"Do you mean nobody will help?"

"Didn't you hear the radio? Maybe it was when you were coming in? Announcer said Palmer Gallery was about to wash away and Pax was gonna lose everything?" His own excitement did not change his speech pattern. He continued to end each sentence with a question mark.

"I'm going over." She grabbed her umbrella.

"Don't be impatient," Bettie Lou said firmly. "Just watch that parking lot." She held onto Freddie's arm. "Watch!" she commanded in a tone that Freddie had never heard her use.

It hurt to see the Bullet taking the brunt of the storm, like a lost animal, stranded on a mountain clearing. As she watched, there was another flash of lightning. All the illumination in the gallery died.

"Look! You must look."

A pickup truck with a homemade tool shed in its bed came into view and nosed slowly into the parking lot. Freddie could see the wake of waves as it eased toward the back.

"Al Jameson and sons must have been close?" Don said.

"What do you mean?"

"Just watch, and thank the good Lord for mountain men?"

She stood transfixed, unmindful of the tears running down her face and soaking her blouse. A parade of rusty pickups converged on the parking lot. Brawny men in overalls and dark work jackets, many with untrimmed beards, climbed out of high cabs, pulled their hats down against the rain and made their way to the gallery. The rain blurred their facial features but they held their shoulders straight.

Something about the way they marched made her know they meant business.

"Pax's friends," Bettie Lou explained. "He has probably done the same, or something similar, for every one of them. He's never let anyone else down, and they've come to help him. There's Eddie, and some men from Montezuma. And I believe that's Arnie Watson from over in Globe Valley. How did they get here so soon? They're coming from everywhere. Don't you recognize anyone?"

"Yes." There was a catch in her throat. "I see Storm and others I know. Where's Don?"

Bettie Lou pointed. He had slipped out without her. She could see Bittle Plumbing on the side of a delivery truck just crossing the highway and turning into the parking lot.

"Help them, God," she said and had never prayed more fervently.

Weave Me a Song

Chapter Twenty-One

In spite of the very real danger, Freddie felt a sense of well-being. The peril was present and real, but it was shared. The hazard had unified neighbors and inspired a community commitment. She counted seven trucks and several cars. She knew that a dozen or more men stood shoulder to shoulder with Pax to nobly fight the ferocious monster that the Linville River had become.

"I wish . . ."

"What?"

"Bettie Lou, where were all those men earlier this week when Pax needed them?"

"They probably didn't know he needed them. I don't imagine many of them even heard of his troubles. But, I think that even if they had known about the horrible – so called – 'exposé,' they would have done nothing."

"Why?" Freddie's voice rose in anger.

"The accusations would be inconceivable to

them. They know Pax. They'd simply dismiss the story as ridiculous gossip. They know what to do today. They can see the danger. They can go in there and use their muscle power and save the inventory by moving it. What could they have done to kill the innuendos and lies?"

"You have a point. I didn't understand. But I *am* grateful for them today."

Bettie Lou broke with her usual practice and kept her radio on the local news station. They spent most of the morning at the front counter, glued to the weather reports. To their immense relief, the weatherman promised that the rains would taper off and the river was predicted to crest by the next morning.

Bettie Lou switched the dial to her gospel music station and the radio poured forth a moving rendition of a church choir.

> *"Shall we gather at the river,*
> *The beautiful, the beautiful river –"*

"Uh, oh." Had Bettie Lou not reached quickly across the counter to the dial and returned to the local station, Freddie might have leaped across the counter and grabbed the dial herself.

Before noon, several of the trucks, as quietly as they had arrived, pulled away from the parking lot. There was no hail and hearty fanfare, merely a dignified withdrawal. Don called to tell them that all the stock had been moved to safety. He was staying a little longer to help secure a lower deck.

Freddie had merely dabbled with her work, and she was standing in the outer office when the back door flew open. For a split second, she did not recognize Pax. He looked like a refugee from a mud wrestling pit.

He was grimy and wild looking. There were dark circles around his eyes and he looked like someone had used a fist to jam his eyes back into their sockets. His lips were parched and cracked. He had a smudge across the bridge of his nose which made it appear as though his nose had been flattened. His posture was stooped with weariness.

She gawked at him. His legs were mud plastered and one pant leg was split half way up to the knee. His jacket and hat were caked in mud, and a dark water was oozing from his boots.

"We've struck gold!" he bellowed, grinning like a chimpanzee.

He's delirious, Freddie thought. That, or he's gone berserk. She guessed his troubles had pushed him over the edge.

He was cradling something in his arms wrapped in plastic and newsprint, safeguarding it as though it were alive. Apparently oblivious of his appearance, or of the mess he was making, he fell to one knee and unwrapped the parcel.

"What on earth?"

"The mystery is solved! *Ta-da!*" He yanked back the protective paper and threw his arms into the air, palms up in a victory gesture. On the floor lay the missing designs and book proposal.

"Pax! Where did you find it?" Freddie knelt on the other side of the package.

"When we had to move one of the file cabinets, it fell from behind it. It had been lodged there for five years."

Bettie Lou had watched quietly. Now, she left the counter and came back to look over the situation. "If that bundle of papers is as important as you two seem to think it is, get it up off the floor. Bring it to the counter. Pax, you poor thing. You look grisly."

Pax scrambled to stuff the papers back into the folder, then checked himself. "These are pretty flimsy. You take them, Fred. I've got to get back to the guys. I don't want them to think I've left them with all the work." He patted the folder and scooped his hands under it and gently lifted it as though he were presenting Freddie with a bouquet of price-less, fragile orchids. "I don't care a thing about the proposal, but check to see if the designs are water-logged. They smell musty. I think there are some outstanding patterns there. The Smithsonian was interested in the older ones." He leaned down to give her a quick kiss. "Honey, when this next night is over, I'm going to sleep for a week. Sorry about the floor, Bettie Lou."

"Now, Pax, don't you worry about it at all."

As soon as the door closed behind him, Bettie Lou was all atwitter. "Proposal? Did I hear that man say proposal?"

Freddie hugged the folder to her breast. She could not control the teasing smile that skipped across her lips. "Yes, he did," she said. She carried the parcel to the counter and gently laid it down. "*Book proposal,* Bettie Lou."

"I thought he was talking about – you know."

Freddie's hands were trembling with excite-ment when she slipped the folder from its wrap-pings and pulled back the top cover to check for damage. The smell of mildew alarmed her. Bettie Lou handed her a roll of paper towels, and she blot-ted the papers as delicately as if they were gold leaf. Some were brittle and yellowed with age. The edges of some were flaking away and reminded her of the delicate scales of a butterfly wing.

Reverence in Freddie's voice gave it a tremor. "See the date? 1894. These were prepared by my great-*great* grandmother." She caressed some small discolored rectangle markings. "Gum tape. Used to fasten them to the loom," she explained.

Bettie Lou watched in awe.

"Look at this one. Garnet Holloway. Gram made this before she was married. She calls them 'drafts.'" She ran her finger across the penciled signature. The sheet of paper seemed as thin as a tissue, as fragile as a snowflake.

Bettie Lou was impressed. "I'm familiar with some weaving patterns, like the 'cup and saucer' or the 'cat paw ' or the 'rose and vine,' but these look different."

"These are Gram's own original designs for her special patterns."

"They look almost like sheet music."

"I guess in a way, they are. Gram makes her loom sing. She'll be so pleased and surprised. She told me once that when she saw a new pattern, she felt just like a musician with a new piece of music. She had to sit right down at her loom and try it out."

"So you could say Pax found *The Lost Chord.*"

"In the composer's own hand."

Weave Me a Song

Chapter Twenty-Two

G*ram's telephone line* was still down. If the rain had slackened, it was not readily discernable, and Freddie's concern for her grandmother grew. She didn't have to be encouraged to leave work early after she was assured that Pax was all right. Elaine and Lamar were taking the evening watch so he could get some sleep. He was confident that the gallery had been spared major damage, and the river would crest by morning.

Most of the houses were still dark, she observed when she turned onto Turkey Hollow Road, and she wondered how soon the electricity would be restored. Gram had assured her she knew how to build a fire and to light the kerosene lamp, and she tried not to worry. The excitement and anticipation of delivering the design folder kept her spirits high. She looked forward to telling Gram about the men of mercy who had come to Pax's rescue.

She parked at the back door. She moved cautiously up the wet stairs, struggling with the umbrella and the screen door. She wished she had not tried to use the dripping paraphernalia, since it slowed her down.

The house was warm and she was reassured. But Gram was not in the kitchen. She pulled off her wet raincoat and draped it across a chair. "Gram?" She found her in her bedroom, rocking and going through some old photograph albums. Freddie saw that her prized cedar chest was open.

The kerosene lamp was not adequate, and she hurried to the storage area on the back porch to find the Coleman lantern. "You'll have to have better light to see what I have for you," Freddie explained.

"Tell me how Pax is." Gram pulled her gray sweater up around her neck.

"You'll never believe that either."

"Oh, I think I will. Storm came out to check on me today. Sed both you and Pax were worried 'bout me. Silly children."

Freddie turned to grin at her. "That old coot came out here?"

"He ain't too bad, once you get used to him. He'll do in a pinch. He stoked up the fire and brought in more wood. Drank up some coffee."

Freddie was surprised to see her grandmother smiling at some secret thought. Setting the lantern on the dresser and spreading the folder out on the bed, she said, "Look what Pax found today."

"I declare! How 'bout that?" She browsed through the papers, stopping occasionally to draw one closer to her eyes and Freddie could hear her quickened breathing. "We still have this one? Child, this is my very first *a-ri-gi-nal* draft. Didn't know we saved that thing. Kind of sloppy." She laid it on the quilt and gently smoothed it out, her hands fluttering across it like a gray moth.

"How old were you when you did it?"

"'Bout thirteen, fourteen. This one was by my grandmother." She picked up another fragile sheet of yellowed paper. "Land's sakes alive!" She sank down on the side of the bed and sorted through the designs. Her weathered hands trembled as she traced the faint pencil markings.

Freddie wished Pax was there to enjoy the pleasure of the old woman. Her diminutive body hardly made an impression in the contour of the bed. "I never saw Pax so excited about anything. He brought them over to me through that hurricane-force rain. He made a terrible muddy mess in the hallway at Bittle's."

"I got something fer you. Been going through my stuff and found a few more drafts. And a few swatches. Mostly of old time patterns. Traditional, I think they call them." She turned back to her cedar chest. "See? This is a sample of the 'honeysuckle' and this here's the 'rose.'"

But Freddie was not looking at the swatches. She knelt beside the cedar chest. "Gram, why do you have all my old sweaters in here?"

"Aw, tish, tish. Meant to have Marge help me move them back to your dresser 'fore you missed them."

"I've been hunting them. Why are they here?"

Gram lowered her eyes and began working her mouth, chewing on her lower lip. "Truth is, child, this is my treasure chest and I keep things that mean a lot to me in here. While you were gone, I wanted something of yours close by. I could reach out and touch them at night. If I got too lonely, I would just spread one 'cross my bed. Land's sake. Must be like an old hound dog who could sniff your presence when something you had worn was nearby."

Freddie shook her head. "I never knew that." Tears, unchecked, slid down her cheeks. "When I called, you never said you were lonely. Your notes always sounded upbeat." Remorse racked her whole being and she trembled. "Gram, how could you love me so? I don't deserve it."

Gram slowly pushed herself up from the bed and moved around to touch Freddie. She gently caressed her cheeks, wiping away the tears and touched her forehead, brushing back her hair. She put her arm around her shoulders and ran her hand up and down her back. "Never thought 'bout it. Just *did* and *do*. Ain't 'specially hard." She chuckled. "You be kinda pretty. 'Course, I could be a mite prejudiced." She eased herself into the rocking chair and continued to stroke Freddie's back. "God give you to me. And God don't give anything that is not holy and good."

"It makes me so ashamed to know the pain I caused you and Pax."

"Hush, now, child. From what I heard, you gave a little joy to Jill and baby Emily Frederica. Maybe they needed you more than Pax and me. At least for that time. Anyway, you got your computing schooling and you *air* home."

"You're quite remarkable, Gram. You've given me unconditional love all of my life and you were more concerned about two people you've never met than you were about yourself. I love you, Gram. I hope I'll grow to be like you. I don't ever want to leave again. I don't want to go any further away than Boone or Asheville."

"Now, now, let's not get plum carried away."

####

Almost as quickly as it started, the flooding stopped, and the river receded. With the sunshine came two remarkable developments in the status of Palmer Gallery.

The Avery Sentinel ran a front page interview with Hilda Olson and carried a scathing editorial denouncing the ethics of one out-of-town reporter.

And Pax received an extraordinary letter from Philip Sloan, editor of *Regional Headline Journal*. "After a telephone conversation with one of your artists, Storm Bartholomew, I did my own investigation as he suggested. As a result, I offer you my profound apology. We do not condone slipshod research and unfair reporting. Nothing justifies the inappropriate writing of Ms. Kim Rosser-Gibson. You will be interested to know that she is no longer associated with us."

Pax cautioned Freddie that their sales had sustained a significant setback and the fair they had worked so hard on had been postponed indefinitely. But he projected a great optimism for full recovery and would be calling Susan back to work soon.

One Saturday he planned to pick Freddie up for an afternoon hike. "I have something to show you and we haven't hiked since you returned."

"We haven't done much of anything for the past several weeks."

"I know, honey. Tell GG to find some glad rags because I've made reservations for us to take Storm to dinner. We need to take care of a little debt of appreciation. Think she'll decline?"

"She won't. She has a surprise for you."

####

Pax had developed the habit of entering through the back door but today Gram positioned Freddie on the front porch as a decoy. She was to usher him into the living room where she would be waiting for him.

He cooperated so readily that Freddie suspected he anticipated the "surprise." He glanced first at the loom and then at GG. The loom was empty and GG was smiling and pointing at the couch. The new weaving had been hemmed and stretched. She had draped it across the back of the couch. A grin split his beard as he surveyed it. He gestured with both thumbs up. "It's a winner, GG."

"Tell Freddie."

He turned to her. "It's a winner, Fred," he repeated. "It is an amazing piece of partnership. I can't tell where one of you stopped and the other started. It has all the Blue Ridge colors and it's your distinctive creation." He stepped back to study it more. "It has changed a little since the first time I saw it. Where's the bright red stripe?"

"What do you mean? When have you seen it before?"

"GG, you scared your granddaughter to death! The first day she was home she came to tell me you'd lost your marbles. I came out to see it then."

"You came out to see it? Where was I?"

"Asleep."

"What?" She stared at them in consternation.

"Gram, I was so devastated by that bizarre color scheme I thought you had gone berserk."

GG snickered. "Worked, didn't it?"

"You had us both worried. Fred, when did

you realize it was a deliberate plot?"

"Not at first. It took me several days."

"You want to explain this to me?" Gram asked. "Do you mean to tell me that I *pretended* to be a blithering old idiot and you each *pretended* to worry 'bout me?"

They nodded their heads in unison, faces serious, eyes solemn, and then they laughed.

GG shook her head. "Sounds plum scary to me, but how else could I have persuaded Freddie to weave again? It worked, though, didn't it?"

"It did indeed. Is this for sale?"

"No," the women answered together and laughed again. "It is our first joint endeavor, Pax. We can't sell it."

"I know the ideal place to exhibit it."

"Are you hard of hearing? It is not for sale."

"I heard you and I agree. I think it should have a place of honor in our living room."

"You're taking a lot for granted." Freddie giggled. "When did you propose? Have I missed something? Maybe I have a hearing problem."

"Details. Details." He swept her off her feet and whirled her around in his arms, no easy feat in the small living room. "I have a witness now. GG, pay attention. Frederica Gouge, I'm asking you to marry me."

"Well . . . " she teased. "Yes, Paxton Palmer, I'll marry you."

Gram brushed her hand across her forehead in mock exasperation. "Whew! I'm glad that is taken care of. I'm tired of all this play acting. Now I don't have to *pretend* to be a blithering idiot no more. I'm going to the kitchen."

Weave Me a Song

Chapter Twenty-Three

He took her hand. She felt the rough warmth of his flesh, and she relaxed and willed her hand into absolute stillness, encased in his, savoring the sense of his protective love.

"Are we taking the Bullet?"

"Let's walk."

She had an urge to dance ahead of him and to spin around and skip back to him. Everything about the day filled her with jubilance, full of song, and she wanted to run and shout. But she craved the closeness of his presence, so she dismissed the impromptu choreography.

He sensed the vitality in her. "You seem full of whoopee and hoopla! I hope it's not restlessness."

She glanced quickly at him. Was there a hint of worry in his voice? "Do you want me to shout hosanna? It is not everyday that someone promises to marry me."

"No?" He beamed at her.

She grew serious. "I've walked around

Gram's property only once since I came home – with the exception of the short walk with Red."

"The photographer? How did he like it?"

"He was especially entranced by the silvery green moss on the sides of the oak trees. He talked about Spanish moss hanging from the old trees in the south, and he was intrigued. He loved the place. Wanted Gram to sell him some land."

"I trust she was uninterested."

She nodded. "See that row of hemlocks? Gram's property goes to there. Let's go up."

The clarity of the day was startling. The rain-cleansed mountains had the glow of a bright new world and the air was fragrant with pungent pine and other sweet conifers. The storm had washed away the last color of fall flowers but Freddie grabbed a handful of fuzzy, curling seed pods of the Sweet Autumn clematis. She pulled back on his arm, to slow him down, and drew his attention to the rhododendrons, some of them taller than he was and loaded with plump sandy-green flower buds.

Further up the hillside, a breeze swept through the hemlocks, sending the slender, drooping branches into a swaying, silver dance. "I love the silver underside of the hemlock needles," Freddie said, and then she froze.

"What's wrong?"

"Shhh. Turn as quietly as you can and look at that beautiful gray fox."

They pivoted together and stared into the brown eyes of the triangle-shaped face of the graceful animal, poised in rapt attention. For a long moment the fox stared, then lifted her aristocratic chin and pranced off down the mountain, her long, bushy black-tipped tail trailing like a bridal train.

"She thinks we're intruding," Pax whispered. "I'll bet she has a den nearby."

"She's the trespasser."

Pax chortled. "*She* is? Why?"

"Because every since I was a small girl, I dreamed of building my house up here."

"Really? How would you handle transportation in the snow and ice?"

"I'd be so much in love with my Prince Charming that we'd stay in our cozy den during the winter. I'd weave and he could do the cooking."

"Really? And what would you do when our four little boys came along?"

She giggled. "Four boys! I want three girls."

"Okay. But remember that the Lord provides the increase."

"Gram and Granddad wanted a house full of children."

They didn't speak for a few minutes, each thinking of Gram. They were out of breath from the climb. He sat down on a big rock at the crest of the hill and pulled her into his arms. "Look at this view."

She snuggled against him. "You can see forever from here." She could see the last tint of lingering summer greenness in the grassy meadows and beyond that, ridge after ridge of deep indigo, fading with each receding view until the blue of the mountain and the sky blended into a single shade. Gram's cottage looked like a dollhouse. Gray smoke curled up from the chimney. Below Gram's she could see Eddie and Susan's house, almost finished. Eddie's truck was there and she knew they had begun to move some furniture in, in preparation for the wedding, less than a month away.

Pax directed her attention back to Gram's

place. "See the grotesque angle of that barn? We need to get that down. It looks like a light dusting of snow would collapse it. Dangerous. Please don't ever go in there."

She looked at the pewter-colored barn, with the sagging tin roof that had rusted to streaks of red-brown in wide, irregular strips. "It's only a harbor for mice and snakes." She shuddered. "I have roofers coming next week for the house."

"I think we better forget that house and build her a suite in ours – right here."

"Here?"

"Could you imagine a log house right here?" he asked.

"It *is* a perfect spot to share with Mrs. Fox."

"I almost sold it to finance the renovations on the gallery."

"Sure you did."

"But my dad talked me out of it."

She twisted around to gape at him. "You're serious. Are you telling me you own this property?"

"I was in the middle of negotiations when – when you left."

She was speechless. She dropped her head and fought tears that blinded her and a tightness in her throat choked her.

"Hush, darling. It's all right now. We still have the land, and we have each other."

She raised her lips to his. When they finally broke the kiss, he took a deep breath.

"We'll have trouble with the access-way. Do you know who owns that strip of property between this and your gram's line?"

"I do." She kissed him again lightly. "But I can tell you it's not for sale. That land belongs to a very stubborn person."

"Most things have a price. Who owns it?"

"I tell you, it's not for sale." She stood and stepped away from him.

He stood up and pulled her into his arms and pressed her close to his heart. "Quit teasing. Who owns it?"

"You couldn't buy it in a hundred years."

"Why?"

She turned away from him and he had to walk around her to face her. She was smiling. "Because I own it. It belonged to my father."

It was his turn to be speechless. He stared at her in open-mouth astonishment.

She slipped her arms under his jacket, enjoying the warmth, and snuggled as close to him as she could get. "Who says dreams don't come true?" She slid her hands all the way to the back of his shoulders, loving every inch of the man. She traced the vertebrae in his spine and felt the rippling in his shoulder muscles as he cuddled her. Her own heart echoed the energetic thumping of his. She shared his passion.

"Fred," he said earnestly and lifted her chin. "I'll love you forever and I pray to God that our marriage will last for the rest of our lives. But it'll be several months before I can even think of building our house."

"I'll wait."

"When we get through this crisis at the gallery – *if* we do – "

"Love is sharing, Pax, the hard as well as the good and we'll get through it together."

"Fred." He smiled and she realized that he could say her silly nickname sensuously, making it sound like a caress.

If he could make "Fred' sound romantic, she had better hang on to him and she told him so.

He laughed and the resonance rolled over the hillside and frightened a pair of mourning doves who took flight in a *whump whump* of whirling wings.

"One other surprise," he said, and his voice was full of rapture. "I hope you'll not insist on a diamond engagement ring."

"I don't need an engagement ring."

"Oh. Okay." He shoved something back into his jacket pocket.

"What do you have?"

He grinned at her. "You helped me mine it."

She looked at him, perplexed.

"When we were in high school, the whole science department took a field trip to the emerald mines near Spruce Pine. Remember?"

"But no one found anything much."

"I did. But I didn't show you. I knew it was your birthstone. I saw an emerald set as a natural crystal years ago and thought it was spectacular. I kept this all these years and decided it might make an unusual engagement ring."

She could hear the slight misgiving in his voice. "We could have it faceted and polished if you prefer, or we could have diamonds added later."

She stared at the breathtaking emerald, set delicately in gold. The gem was a hexagonal prism, set at an angle, and the color was an astounding green. "It's the most fabulous ring I've ever seen. It sings of the mountains, yet it came from the darkest depths of the earth. I love it."

His face was filled with tenderness. "The color is the important thing to appraise in an emerald. This one's very green."

"It's perfect. Did you design it?"

"I had help from the goldsmith," he admitted. "Now, don't start crying."

"Crying?"

"Women do the strangest things. Both you and my mother cry over almost anything. Even beautiful things. Must be a female thing."

"I'd never cry," she said and sniffed. "Just because I have the sniffles and I'm the happiest person in the world. Do you have a handkerchief?"

He laughed and pulled one from his pocket, and she knew he had planted it there for her.

Chapter Twenty-Four

*F*reddie stared at Gram and wondered. Something was . . . different. She was not particularly alarmed, merely baffled. For days Gram had demonstrated a strange secretiveness. It was not especially erratic, but it was different. She seemed flustered when Freddie came home early one day, and she kept the door to her bedroom closed. Nothing criminal in that, but out of the ordinary, nevertheless. Finally, she simply assumed that Gram was probably working on a Christmas mystery, and that thought brought back memories of similar actions when she was a child.

But one evening she was surprised to find her grandmother hard at work in the living room when she got home from work.

"I've measured the warp for a new weaving," she confessed, and she looked like the cat that had swallowed the canary.

Freddie was astounded. "How could you do that? How did you manage your warping board and how did it get here?"

Gram had the grace to blush. "Storm," she explained. "Wal, Marge has been helping me, too. We have already 'chained' the yarn." She pointed to a wicker basket near the loom.

Freddie saw yards and yards of linen yarn loosely wound, already carefully measured and tied in two-yard intervals, or "chained", as Gram mentioned, to keep it from getting full of knots. She shook her head in disbelief. "I guess Storm brought the warping board down from the storeroom."

"Yep,"

"But how can you beam the loom? That's a job for three people at least! Who'll crank?"

"That's where you come in."

"You and I can't do it alone."

"No, ain't 'specting us to. But both Storm and Marge are willing to come help us Saturday. But Storm is expecting to stay for lunch, the sly old coot."

Freddie laughed. "If you're able to do all this work, something tells me I need to find another loom for myself."

"You got a loom."

"No, Gram. You're going to get back to this one. I know it. Look how you've improved already."

Gram sat down and hooked her cane over the back of her chair. "Wal, Storm and I been discussing it. There is a fine old loom out in the loft of the barn. Old as the hills, and got a few pieces missing, but Storm thinks he can carve whatever pieces we need. We been kinda planning on the project as a wedding gift. Next time Pax is here, you and he can take a look at it. But be careful in that old barn."

# # # #

"Who is that in the truck with Pax?"

Gram raised her chin and strained to adjust her bifocals. "Don't know."

Whoever it was sat serenely in the passenger seat until Pax opened his door and stepped out. The passenger slid over to the driver's seat and then jumped to the ground behind Pax.

"I declare. Pax has a dog," Gram said, her voice hiking with interest.

The black, white and tan Sheltie stood obediently at attention until Pax closed the door. He pranced gracefully beside Pax as they approached the house. He waited with quiet dignity, regarding Freddie through the screen door with reserved composure until she stepped out onto the front porch. He gave Pax an inquiring glance and then lost his restraint as she knelt to welcome him. He came to her arms as though it were a reunion. "Pax?"

"Fred, meet Sir Francis Drake. Sir Francis for short."

Sir Francis's dignity dissolved as he explored Freddie's face, his nose quivering. She looked into his large round eyes and caressed the smooth short hair on his lean muzzle. She inspected his black ears that were set like a pair of furry wings. She stroked the long, straight hair of his outer coat. The undercoat of his white chest was short and furry and his whole body shone like silk. He gave one plaintive whimper, beseeching her acceptance.

"He needs a home," Pax explained quietly. "He's completely trained, but his owner is having to give him up."

"How come?" Gram asked succinctly from the doorway.

"Getting too old."

"The dog or the owner?" Gram queried.

Freddie continued to kneel beside the dog, getting acquainted.

"The owner, but Sir Francis is no pup. He's sturdy and intelligent enough to patrol both homes. Mr. Carey has to give up his house and move to a retirement center. Sir Frances needs plenty of roaming space. He's a registered Shetland sheepdog."

"Looks like a runt of a collie to me."

As if on cue, Sir Francis turned his attention to GG. He raised his big brown eyes to her, and Freddie swore later, his black and tan face broke into a grin. He whined and lifted a paw, showing his gentlemanly manners and waited patiently until GG had transferred her cane to her left hand. Giggling like a school girl, she shook his extended appendage.

"Wal, land's sake. I had one like you when I was a girl. Didn't call him no 'Sir', though. But don't be a tripping me, dog."

Pax said, simply, "I have his bed in the truck."

"Best put it in the kitchen," was GG's only comment.

They sauntered, laughing and holding hands, toward the barn. Sir Francis danced around their feet like the swirling foam of the sea surf until Pax gave him a stern command, "Heel." When the dog obeyed, Pax said more gently, "Careful, lad, you'll trip us and neither of us has time for a broken leg."

"Look! Snowflakes! Our first snow. You said a light dusting would knock the old barn down."

"It's a beautiful barn, in spite of its lop-sided slant. Must have been magnificent in its day." All at once, he stopped so suddenly that his abrupt halt jerked her back against him. "You know what? I have a great idea. Look at that wood! Must be well over a hundred years old, maybe more than that."

"Isn't it rotten?"

"Not the outside siding. Do you have any idea what rough sawn siding is worth? That weathered wood could make fantastic paneling in a family room or studio."

She glanced at him. "Could we recycle it?"

"Sure, Why not? That stuff would cost a fortune if we tried to buy it. I'd rather have chestnut, but this pine will do beautifully. Haven't been any chestnut trees in years."

"Why?"

They were all wiped out in a blight nearly a hundred years ago." He waved a hand at the surrounding woods and back to the barn. "We can take the barn down and use that wood."

"But how?"

"Honey, in case you haven't noticed, you're marrying an ox. I'm as strong as a mule. I'll tear it down with my bare hands." He flexed his muscles and emitted a guttural grunt.

Sir Francis responded with a growl, and Freddie giggled. "I think it's a wonderful idea," she said. Joy rushed through her, and she tingled all over. She wasn't sure she could handle much more happiness. Breaking away from him, she called her dog and raced ahead in a running romp. The Sheltie went crazy with pleasure, twisting his body in exotic side stepping, that would seem to break his back. The expression of merriment in Pax's eyes reflected the excitement she felt – like a little kid.

Snowflakes swirled around them, and suddenly the sun broke through the clouds, and the air seemed filled with sparkling confetti. "You're being dusted in diamonds." he chuckled.

"My friends in Arizona thought I was fibbing when I told them that it sometimes snows here when the sun is shining. No one would believe me."

"Well, perhaps it'll be snowing when Jill and Emily come for the wedding."

"I hope they can come." She was pensive a moment before she continued. "You know, Pax, using the old wood will give us a sense of family continuity. I'll go tell Gram and see what she thinks. I know she'll be pleased. It'll remind her of her Del."

####

Gram stared at Freddie in surprise, then grabbed her cane and a sweater. "Wal, land's sakes. Why didn't we think of that? I nearly had that barn burned down while you were gone. I'll come take a look with you."

The two women walked back toward the barn more slowly. By the time they reached it, Pax was already climbing the ladder to the loft.

"Careful, son," Gram admonished as they paused to let their eyes adjust to the dimness within the barn. "That ladder could be rot – "

She never completed the sentence.

There was a sharp warning crack as the ladder rung gave way and then a scraping sound as Pax flayed his feet against the ladder, groping for another step. Fred saw him reach up, grappling, for a handhold. He seemed to hang in space a second, then, with a handful of straw, he plunged.

It was in slow motion, burned forever in her memory, the big man raising his arms, and sliding down through the horrible height of dark expanse, feet first, toes pointed down, jacket flaring out from his sides – down, down, down, falling helplessly, She wanted to run to try to catch him or to cushion his fall, but she stood paralyzed with fear.

She never heard the impact. She caught a searing glimpse of a pain-wracked grimace and saw dust rising – and the crunched, horrible heap of Pax. There was no sound, only the frozen, void deadness of absolute paralysis.

It was like her nightmares when she was unable to breathe or move. She seemed to crawl to him, in some kind of drugged state, calling his name and begging him to respond. She sank beside him not daring to touch him, and resisted the desire to pull his head against her breast.

"Back hurts," he mumbled, and she knew he was alive.

"Run, child. Call 911."

"I can't – "

"Go."

The command gave her impetus.

She thought she heard him moan. And she ran as she had never run in her life.

Weave Me a Song

Chapter Twenty-Five

She would wonder, later, if the shock – and the anesthesia it produced – was a blessing. But now, kneeling beside Pax, straining to hear the sound of the ambulance siren, concentrating on it, trying to *will* its approach, she knew she was *dying* because she thought he was.

She could hear Gram praying, and Sir Francis' gentle whine as he nosed Pax, and then she heard a weak moan. "Pax!" She was weeping now and she touched his forehead, knowing she must not move him. "Sweetheart."

He didn't turn his neck and she could hardly hear him, but there was a hoarse, rasping whisper, "I broke my back."

"Shh! The ambulance is coming." She stroked his beard, staying as close to him as she dared, feeling the reassurance of his breath against her cheek. An eon of time passed. When she heard Sir Francis barking, she knew the rescue squad had come.

They moved her out of the barn as they cared for him, the volunteer members of the local emergency team. Gram stayed with her and it was the older, bent woman who held and sustained the younger one.

When they had safely transferred him to the ambulance, they let her speak to him. "I'm going too," she said and she clung to him. In the end, they broke the rules and let her ride in the front passenger seat. The seatbelt kept her from flying to the floor as she was jostled from side to side when the driver maneuvered the sharp mountain curves on his way to Linville. The noise of the siren was deafening. It was a relief when they were close enough to the hospital to turn it off.

She waited quietly, meekly staying out of their way as they carried Pax on the back board through the swinging emergency room doors, away from her. Standing alone at the entry, she was vaguely reassured by their speed and efficiency. She was a lost waif, staring at the doors:

"EMERGENCY ONLY

NO ADMITTANCE."

In a daze, completely disoriented, she wondered where to wait. The snow came down, but she no longer felt the kiss of diamond dust. She was suddenly very, very cold.

An attentive nurse saw her and led her gently to the waiting room. "You wait here. We'll call you just as soon as you can see him."

She was dimly aware of the movements and sounds of the busy staff but they seemed far away and she remained hunched low in the chair, just as wretched now as she had been gloriously happy less than an hour before. *I can't think,* she said to herself, and that also was a blessing because she could not reflect on all that might have been.

Half in a trance, she looked up to see Don Bittle and then Susan and Eddie. She leaned against Susan and cried.

# # # #

Don escorted her to the door of the emergency room when the nurse called, but she went in alone. She was acutely aware of the smell of antiseptic as she made her way past curtained beds. At the last bed in the ward, a male nurse pulled back the curtains to let her see Pax. He looked better than she expected and he gave her a wane smile. She rushed to his side. "How are you? Are you in lots of pain?"

"Some." He squeezed her hand. "It's better. The orthopedic guy is in surgery. Honey, you've got to promise me that – "

"No."

Frowning, he continued in a barely audible voice. "You don't know what I am going to say."

"I know. I know you, Pax." She pinned him back to the bed with a hand on each shoulder. "I'm not going to let you out of this engagement, no matter what."

"I may never walk again."

"Maybe. But you *will* be my husband. I have a witness who heard you ask me to marry you."

He stared at her. "But – "

"Pax, listen to me, and you listen good." The sternness in her own voice shocked her but he watched her in silence. "You told me once that no one has to merit love. I love you now and even if you never walk again, I'll love you."

He looked away from her and tried to

chuckle, but the sound stuck in his throat. "But what about kids?"

"They'll love you too."

He shook his head. "Honey, honey, honey," he whispered, "you know what I mean. What if – "

"Hush." She silenced his lips with her kiss.

They were interrupted by a lab technician. "I need to get more blood, Mr. Palmer."

"I'll go call Gram. And your parents. Do you want to see Don or Eddie or Susan? They're all in the waiting room."

#

The pain woke him. His back hurt horribly but he could not keep his legs still. He thrashed about, shoving his right leg down the mattress and then his left leg. He twisted slightly in the small bed, but there was no relief. Where was he? Why did he feel the need to whisper?

He opened his eyes and glanced around the dimly lit room. Then he saw her, and it all came back to him – the pain like a red hot poker jammed up his spine when he fell – and the panic. He knew instantly that his back was broken, and he had a fleeting image of himself chained to a wheelchair for the rest of his life. He wiggled his toes and thanked God there was not total paralysis.

Fred slept, all curled up, in the chair that was obviously uncomfortable. She looked like a little street urchin, and suddenly he felt a lump in his throat. She had been there all night. She had climbed right into the ambulance and refused to let it go without her. Spunky little critter.

Emotion welled up within him, threatening to take over. Shoot, if he was going to cry he should save it until his mom got here. He brought his attention back to Fred. She looked a sight, and if it didn't hurt so much he would have mustered a smile. She had come with him without a heavy coat or even a comb. No running back to the house to get a purse or lipstick for her.

He loved her so much it make a hard knot in his chest. He wondered if she understood the depth of his devotion. He believed, with all his heart, that if a man truly loved a woman, he made her his wife and *then* he made love to her, committing his life and fidelity to her. He hoped she understood, but when he tried to explain, it sounded, by today's standards, sticky sweet and sick-sounding *gobbly-gook*. She had touched his lips and whispered, "That's part of the reason I love you so much." He had wondered if that had contributed to her leaving before, but he knew better than that now.

What in God's name was he having this dialogue with himself in the early morning hours in a hospital bed before he knew for sure he would ever walk again – or be able to make love?

The sight of her, crumpled in that chair in his hospital room made the longing throb within him in spite of the intense pain, which was growing intolerable. He rang for the nurse.

The injection eased his pain. He closed his eyes and reviewed the crucial day. He had hunted for weeks for the right dog. Owning a dog would demonstrate, to Fred and to her grandmother, Fred's commitment to stay. It would separate her from her mother's behavior. He remembered the confession in the orchard, and suffered again for his stupidity because of the telephone call he heard her make. It was a wonder he had not lost her forever then.

Finding the right dog for her would make up for some of his insensitivity that day he had been so insufferably foolish. He knew a pup would be too feisty for GG, so he had been hunting an older, better trained dog. He had met Sir Francis when he had delivered a sculpture to Mr. Carey's home. When he heard that the older man was relocating, he played a hunch.

It was worth all his efforts when Freddie saw the Sheltie. As soon as she knelt to greet him, Pax knew it was a conquest. And GG had surrendered without protest. He didn't even have to deliver the little pep talk he had prepared for GG. He felt jubilant when Fred romped with the dog, acting more like herself, more like the old Fred he remembered.

He had ruined it all when he fell in that dumb barn. One more stupid mistake. He should have checked the ladder more carefully, but the lower rungs had been sound enough. Maybe they should have just burned the barn.

The medication was making him sleepy. . . .

It was barely daybreak when Freddie woke up, conscious of the presence of a physician dressed in a green scrub suit. Apparently, he had been talking quietly with Pax for several minutes.

"Miss Gouge," he acknowledged. "I've been in surgery most of the night and just had a chance to study the X-rays. I don't often make calls this early but I knew Pax would be impatient."

He turned to address Pax. "It's not as bad as it could have been," he began, "but you have compressed fractures of the lumbar vertebrae one and two. You'll have to be here a week or so at least, and then go into physical therapy. You'll be laid up another six or eight weeks, if everything goes well. It was a close call."

"I knew it was a broken back."

"Pax, I don't have to tell you that you are mighty lucky. You say you fell about sixteen feet? Could have been paralyzed for life. And, listen, young man, a wrenching fall in the next few months could result in serious, permanent spinal injury, possibly paralysis. No more ladders! No heavy work of any kind – that foundation may have to wait. You'll have to make some arrangements for your gallery for awhile. Can your partner handle it by herself?"

Pax said, "Actually, we haven't had much business lately."

"So I heard. Bad break. Excuse the pun."

After he left Freddie said, "You were discussing our new house with him?"

"I had to explain the compromising position you put me in."

"What are you talking about?"

"He knew I'd spent the night with a beautiful woman."

Weave Me a Song

Chapter Twenty-Six

S*he woke up* in terror, trembling and drenched with sweat. Had she screamed out in her sleep? Something soft and damp nudged her hand. She heard Sir Francis whimpering and she became wide awake. Had he sensed her fear and climbed the stairs to her room?

Had she experienced another nightmare? She couldn't remember. A soft light from a full moon flooded her bedroom and she could see the clock on her night stand. Three A.M.

Was something wrong with Pax? Was Gram all right? Something was horribly awry, something evil enough to wake her from a deep sleep.

Tired to the point of exhaustion when Susan had brought her home, Freddie had given Gram a quick update on Pax's condition and tumbled into bed. She had not slept well at the hospital and she was asleep in her own bed by the time her head hit the pillow. But some terror had awakened her. She lay absolutely still and listened for a clue. Had her cries in the throes of a nightmare brought Sir Francis up the stairs from his bed in the kitchen?

She got out of bed and slipped on her robe. Perhaps he had come to summon her for Gram! Stealthily, with Sir Francis at her heels, she crept down the stairs in the dark. Gram's nightlight gave enough illumination that she could see her sleeping peacefully, chest rising and falling rhythmically.

Halfway back up the stairs, she wondered where she had stored her suitcase, and then she remembered. The overwhelming frustrations. The need to escape.

Pax, in considerable pain after his tests, had grown cross and impatient during the day. Her own fatigue and concern hadn't helped, but the burden of his care hung heavily on her. It would be a couple of days before his parents could get there to take over the responsibility. The whole scenario was folding in on her, like a millstone around her neck.

It had been dark when Susan offered her a ride home. She remembered noticing, as she walked through the living room, that Gram's loom looked naked, waiting for her help in the strenuous beaming process. She had promised to do it before the accident, but, she thought impatiently, she couldn't manage everything.

Sir Francis whined again, and she wondered if he needed to go outside, but he walked to her bed, dropped down on the rug next to it and curled up, continuing to follow her every move with large, concerned eyes. She had not had time to develop a relationship with him; she hadn't had time to change clothes or to eat a decent meal.

Suitcase. She sank down on the side of the bed. The fear had subsided, but a terrible dread of facing tomorrow became a dark oppression. She wanted to crawl back into bed and disappear. She wanted to fly away. She felt totally defeated and inadequate.

Shame stung her eyes. The dream that woke her was unlike the nightmares involving Brad and Phoenix. She had been packing her suitcase, preparing to flee.

She slung her legs over and across the bed and slid to the other side where she could see out the window. She had to lean forward to see the top of the mountain where she and Pax planned to build their house.

"Oh, my God. I was planning to run away." She covered her face with her hands and tried to muffle her sobbing. Sir Francis came around the bed and pressed gently against her leg. She had been contemplating running away in her sleep. Was her mother's demon taking over her life?

She trembled all over. She felt dirty and rotten and worthless. For a long time she stayed motionless. She couldn't even pray for help. She deserved no help.

Then, a rasping shaky voice came to her as she remembered Gram's favorite scripture, and she could hear her grandmother quote Psalms 121:
I will lift up my eyes unto the hills, from whence cometh my help. My help cometh from the Lord.

She said it aloud, deliberately, hesitantly, her voice catching. Sir Francis listened, but he was not critiquing her prayer.

Gradually, she relaxed, and an incredible peace spread through her. *God, help me,* she prayed silently. She studied the mountains, and the realization that she and Pax would build a house there created shivers of joy. She loved him, and he loved her. With that kind of love, they could face the world together. *Together.* That was the key. Was the singing in her heart loud enough to wake Gram?

A tremendous sense of victory filled her. She had faced the demon, and she knew she would never run away again. She was not alone. *Thank you, Lord,* she whispered. She lay back down and slept soundly.

It's a shame, she thought, that they couldn't give him an injection that would handle the discouragement as easily as the one that reduced the pain. She wondered why, with a broken back, he continued to thrash about in the bed. When she asked the nurse about it, she told her it could be due to nerve damage and that it was totally out of Pax's control. It was better, she told herself, than paralysis.

Pax had never been an idle man. Now, confined to bed, pumping his restless legs, he had little to do but to think about the catastrophes at the gallery and his inability to do anything about them now.

He told her he was not sure that Elaine, even with Susan called back to work, could handle all the problems. Kim Rosser-Gibson had done her best to destroy them, and that disaster was followed by the flood. He lay helpless in bed, he complained, and the doctor said it would be months before he could get back to his full work load.

"The future was so bright a few weeks ago," he said sadly.

"The future is still bright. You've been put on a side track, not derailed."

"Can't even get married."

She bristled. "Why not?" she demanded. "I thought we had settled that."

"Don't have a place to live."

"Millions of people get married with a whole lot less than we have. We could live with Gram."

He stared at her. "I can't climb stairs." His tone was flat and listless and she knew it was useless to argue.

The third day after the accident, Freddie returned to work for a few hours. When she hurried back to the hospital, she found Pax's parents in his room. She could not remember her own mother, and her father had been dead half of her life. The only family she had was her grandmother, and she wondered how she would relate to his family. She entered the room with a few qualms. She had been in high school the last time she had been around the Palmers.

She had not realized, fully, the extent of her distress over Pax's accident or the burden of the responsibility in caring for him. When her future mother and father-in-law welcomed her with open arms, she dissolved into tears.

"I told you," Pax said, and laughed.

"Just like your mother," Paul Palmer agreed.

"She is a lot like mother, in many ways."

"I knew I liked her very much."

Barbara Palmer continued to grasp Freddie's hand. "You look exhausted," she said. "I'm sorry we could not get here sooner but Paul had trouble finding a substitute. There are not too many who can teach advanced Latin."

####

When Freddie took the Palmers out to the

house to see Gram, Storm Bartholomew was there. He was getting ready to investigate the barn and Paul, Freddie and Sir Francis joined him.

Storm pointed to the old barn. "The boy wants to use that siding. Rough sawn pine. Plans to use it as paneling in his family room or studio."

"The outside siding? Isn't that unusual?"

"Yep. Your son has an eye for the unusual. Reason his gallery is so successful. But I have to see about something GG is fussing about."

They paused at the entrance of the barn. Paul shook his head. "I don't want Barbara to see this. Is that where my boy fell?" He grimaced. "What was he doing trying to get into the loft?"

"That was my fault, I guess," Storm said. "There was an old loom stored up there at one time. Del and I put it up there. I wanted to fix it up for Freddie as a wedding gift."

"It's not that important," Freddie said. "Nothing is important enough for someone else to risk getting hurt."

"Wal, now Garnet thinks that Del moved the loom to the old storage shed on the back side of the building."

Freddie led the way around to the shed. Storm unlatched the door and they pulled it open. It was dim and dusty inside, but there in the middle of the shed lay the bundled pieces of an antique loom. Around the walls were stacks and stacks of lumber.

"If that ain't the cat's whiskers." Storm picked up a board and examined it, took off his hat and ran a hand across his brow. "Chestnut. Must be two, three thousand board feet."

"I didn't know there was that much fine chestnut left in the whole country," Paul said.

"Pax said that a blight had killed the trees," Freddie said.

"Yep," Storm said, looking at her. The master woodcarver explained. "Think it was an Asian fungus blight. Took over in about 1904, and in forty years, warn't a grown tree standing."

"That's why it's so valuable."

"Right purty wood to begin with. Rich color and beautiful graining. I got a contractor friend who would rob a gold-mine to buy this."

"This wood might make it possible for us to start our house sooner."

Paul held up a hand in caution. "No, hold on. I can tell you what Pax will say. He'll say that this belongs to GG."

Freddie laughed. "Let's go see what Gram has to say about it. But I think I know what she'll say. She nearly had this barn burned down just to get rid of the dilapidated thing before it fell down. I think if she hadn't remembered about the loom, she would have. She'll probably say: 'Sonny boy, if you care one thing about my feelings and what I can give you, you'll take it and be smart.'"

#

They stood at the foot of Pax's bed, all of them, and Storm said, "Pax, my boy, we have some news to cheer you up while you are lying here in bed drawing house plans."

"Why would I be drawing house plans when it'll be months and months before we can raise the money to begin to build?"

Paul smiled. "Let GG tell you."

"Got a little wedding gift fer you. Show him

the sample, Storm. Got a shed full of the stuff. Storm thinks it's worth a right smart o' money, too."

Pax gaped at the wood. "A shed full of chestnut? Where?"

"Jest other side of the barn. I kin barely remember Del's dad storing that. Plum forgot about it. Yours to use or to sell."

Pax pulled himself higher in the bed. He ran his hand over the grain of the wood. "This sample hasn't even been through the planer and look at the beauty. It's fabulous, GG, but I can't touch it. It belongs to you."

Freddie looked at her future father-in-law. She saw the facial muscles in his jaw working, as he tried to hold back laughter. He didn't have to wait long for Gram's blistering tirde.

"Sonny boy, ain't you got no regards fer my feelings? Don't be high-handed with me. I don't have much to offer fer a wedding gift but you could have the gumption to take what I have to offer and be gracious enough to thank me!"

Both Storm and Paul roared with laughter. They had to explain their reaction.

Pax had the grace to accept the inevitable. "I thank you kindly, ma'am, and I promise to build your granddaughter the best house I am capable of building." He held his hand out to Freddie.

Gram slapped her hands together. "All right. Do it."

"One of these days, " Pax told Freddie later, "I'm going to have to hire some high priced computer whiz to set up my accounting program."

"I know a good one, but she isn't cheap."

His laughter filled the room. "You know what? I'll have to get on the road and do some scouting for new work. Elaine and Susan are selling everything in stock. How would you like to go backpacking in the mountains for our honeymoon?"

"I'd love to know all your artists."

"I'll show you some of the prettiest spots in the in the whole Blue Ridge Mountains and we'll wander over into the Smokies, too." He described some of his favorite people. "Way up near the peak of Roan Mountain I know a silversmith who's a crackerjack with gem stones. And I have to take you down to the Piedmont to show you off to some of the finest potters in the country."

It was ludicrous to think of him as exploiting an artist, she thought again.

"How is Sir Francis doing?" he asked just before she left for the night.

"I have bad news for you. You're going to have to get me another dog."

A frown darkened his face. "What happened to Sir Francis?" He tried to pull himself up onto his elbows and winced.

She grimaced at his pain. "Nothing's wrong, exactly. What I mean is, I think I've lost him."

"How? Where?"

" Gram. She's fallen in love with him. I think they bonded together since I have spent so much time here at the hospital with some man I know."

He grinned. "Does she let him sleep in the kitchen?"

"She keeps his bed in her room, right next to her bed except for the night . . ." She tried to retreat but he was wary and had been watching her closely.

"From the sadness in your face, I'd guess you had another nightmare. My God, honey, I thought you were through with those."

She came to stand beside him and made herself busy smoothing down the collar of his pajamas. "Tell me," he insisted.

She shared with him the terrible dream. "I must have called out, because Sir Francis bounded up the stairs. But, Pax, I faced that demon. I know I will never run away again."

"My precious one," he said as he pulled her down to his lips, "you are so easy to love."

Chapter Twenty-Seven

Gram's gift had a remarkable jumpstarting effect on Pax. He littered his bed with house drawings and estimates, and he kept his calculator humming.

"How do you like this?" he asked when Freddie arrived after work. He handed her a detailed drawing.

"Did you do this? I had no idea you were so talented."

He had rendered a plan for the living room, showing wainscoting with a decorative chair rail. "I know what I want, and I'm a very stubborn man. I work until I get it. I thought the chestnut would be a little dark so the upper part of the room will be wall board. Storm wants to cut the chair rail, with an artistic molding. But it all depends on your approval."

"You flatter me, honey. I don't know about all this. I think it's beautiful, but you and Storm know more about it than I do. I also suspect you'll get lots of help with the house."

When news of Pax's injury spread through the community, he was besieged with visitors, all of them eager to offer promises of help when he began building their house. One offer that especially pleased him was from a gifted stone mason. "I'll help you build the nicest fireplace you'll ever see," he promised, "if you'll let me forage granite off your property."

"Fair exchange," Pax agreed.

One day Freddie found his drawings filed neatly in a folder, completed and ready for the builder. He was busy with another project, but he became reticent and self-conscious when she leaned over to observe what he was working on.

"May just be a pipedream," he explained. "I keep thinking of GG's wonderful designs. I discovered that Storm has some original patterns of old works, and I've been doing some research. While I'm lying around for the next few months, I am going to work on a history of some of the crafts of the Blue Ridge."

"Oh, Pax!"

Freddie hated to attend Susan and Eddie's wedding without Pax, but Gram put on her nicest dress and went with all the excitement of a teenager. Looking around at the guests, Freddie was amazed at how dear so many friends had become to her since her return. Elaine and Lamar, Bettie Lou and Don, and of course, Susan and Eddie. Pax was to have been best man, but Don was standing in his place with the groom at the altar.

When the congregation stood as the organist began the wedding march, tears filled Freddie's eyes. She had never attended a wedding without becoming misty-eyed when the bride appeared. The ceremony was sacred and meaningful to her. Susan was glowing, and Freddie remembered the pain she had felt for the few days she thought Pax was engaged to her. She fingered her engagement ring, and a smile tugged at her mouth.

Susan was a beautiful bride, graceful and dream-eyed. She made a regal entrance, causing both Freddie and Gram to catch their breath.

"Trouble is," Freddie said later to Pax, "I kept seeing another couple up there getting married."

He grinned. "It'll be a while."

"Why?"

He groaned. "Not again! You know I refuse to marry you until I'm able to build our house and take care of you."

"I looked up the meaning of your name, Paxton. It means 'peace.' Yet, every time we talk about our wedding, we get into a quarrel."

"Takes two to fight. Honey, you come in here all dewy-eyed about Susan's wedding. I want you to have the kind of memories of our wedding that Susan has of hers."

"The only people I truly want at my wedding are you and Gram. I won't notice anyone else. Of course, if your folks could come, I'd like that."

"And my sisters and your friends from Arizona. No, you'll want the whole shooting match. I'll not deny you that."

"But, Pax . . . "

Susan delayed a honeymoon in order to help Elaine at the gallery, and the daily bulletins from there were encouraging. They were rapidly recovering from the slump that had followed the infamous news story.

Freddie had spent most of her after-work hours at the hospital, but the strain was telling on her. She had neglected her grandmother, and she was eager to begin another weaving.

She would not have complained, however, except that Pax was getting impatient. He tired of his drawings and complained about physical therapy.

"I want to go home," he said.

"I know. I'll see you tomorrow." She had grown weary of arguing with him. "I'm going to take Sir Francis for a long walk before it gets dark."

She ignored the disappointment in his eyes.

Chapter Twenty-Eight

 $Dr.$ *Seller was in Pax's* room. Trying not to intrude, Freddie waited at the door and listened until he sensed her presence and inclined his head in her direction, including her. "I guess you heard me say that he can go home early next week if he has someone to care for him. I had hoped that his parents would be able to stay awhile."

"He could come to our house, except there are lots of stairs."

"I don't think that would be wise just yet. In a month or so, he could manage stairs but they would be painful to him now. He needs to go back to his apartment, only – "

Freddie sighed. "He needs to marry me and let me take care of him, but he's too stubborn."

Pax sputtered. "Now, Fred."

Dr. Sellers laughed. "I'm a physician, not a marriage counselor, so I'll stay out of this."

Pax looked sadly at her when the doctor left. "You've got to see it my way, Fred. I can't even get my trousers on by myself and forget about my shoes and socks! I'll not be humiliated by having you attend to me. I'm just too independent to adjust to that. I'd feel like you had custody of me."

"You let the nurses and the aides help you."

"I'm not married to them. Anyway, my apartment is too small for two people."

"I thought that was what marriage was all about – intimacy." She walked to the window and stood with her back to him. "You talk about humiliation. I think a little humility might be a credit to you." She stared at the mountains a long time and let him stew, and then she said quietly, "I thought you loved me."

"I do love you, honey, that's why I can't – "

She whirled around, eyes blazing. "You said you were stubborn and boy, you are! Maybe a little selfish too. You love me only if you can be strong and macho. If *you* can be the caregiver. It would be okay for me to be indisposed but not you. You want to hold me and chase away my nightmares, but you don't want me to share your pain. You want to build a room for Gram in *your* house, but you are too darned proud to stay in *her* house. Love is a two-way street, Pax. Why would it be so shameful to have a wife help you dress, or drive you?"

"A man is supposed to take care of his wife."

"And you will, eventually. Can't you get it through your thick head that this condition is temporary? And even if it wasn't, I want to be with you and to – well, do anything that needs to be done."

He pounded his clenched fist on the clipboard beside him and the intensity of his emotion startled her. "You'll rob me of my . . . manhood!"

She studied him, frowning, her brows knitted in thought. When she spoke, her voice was quiet and sad. She was on the verge of tears, and her dark eyes were filled with weariness. "No. I want nothing of the kind. I thought you loved me unconditionally. You don't. You love me only in health. The marriage vows read 'sickness and health.'" As she talked she raised her outstretched hands, palms up, toward him in a pleading gesture. She dropped them to her sides now. She spun around and left the room so silently that he did not hear her footsteps on the terrazzo hospital floor.

####

Pax lay completely still. Misery washed over him like a soot-colored thunderhead swallowing Grandfather Mountain. He had been trying to consider her, wanting to protect her, spare her. She had a lot of nerve. He was not going to lie around and let his *bride* help him with all the problems of living as a semi-invalid. He could not imagine letting her help him dress, and all the other details like driving the car and opening doors for him.

He wanted to take care of *her*. He was a big, strong man and she was a tiny little wisp of a thing. He had planned a honeymoon she would never forget – and she wanted to spend the honeymoon nursing him. Well, forget it. A man had his pride.

He closed his eyes tightly but he couldn't get the image of her out of his mind – the sorrowful expression in her face, the pain in her eyes. He had hurt her so terribly once before when he incorrectly assumed she was leaving, and now he had done it again. He did not deserve her. She had faced the demons in her life. Maybe he had one to face. Stubbornness she had called it. Perhaps it was false pride.

He gritted his teeth and made his decision. He did a slow roll to the edge of the bed. ("Imagine yourself a log," the therapist had directed.) He pulled his legs up and then, taking a deep breath, he braced himself on an elbow. Slowly, he pushed the upper part of his body up as he kept his back in alignment, slid his feet over the side of the bed, and shifted into a sitting position. Whew! Perhaps the worst was over. Getting up and down was the hardest part, and he had never done it alone before.

The pain was bad, but bearable. Good thing he had long arms, he thought as he reached for the walker. He grabbed the handles and drew it toward him. Gradually, he transferred his weight to his legs and stood up, pausing to let the pain subside and to steady himself. He should have made two telephone calls before he got out of bed He bit his tongue and stood as he placed the first call.

He started out of the room, then retreated and pressed the call button. He had to have help getting into his robe.

####

What if she had already left the hospital? Her coat was still hanging on the back of the chair in his room. He knew she sometimes went to the waiting room while a nurse or an aide cared for him, so he headed that way, shoving his walker ahead of him, taking infant steps. Painfully, he progressed down the long corridor, moving at a snail's pace, aware of the polished floors, the stark white walls broken only by framed portraits of smiling staff members. Pungent antiseptics, lemon-scented furniture polish, and the early supper trays with stainless steel dome-covered plates, vied for prominence. For a moment, he felt nauseted.

Fred didn't look up as he clumped into the room. She sat with shoulders hunched, legs curled up under her body, hands pressed against her drooping forehead. An arrangement of dried hydrangea sat stiffly on the coffee table, its pinks and blues only a faded memory of summer brilliance. She seemed pale as the flowers, as drained of vitality.

He knew then that he loved her more than his own pride, more than life itself. If it took humility on his part, he would develop it. He took a big gulp as he moved to within a foot of her chair.

His voice was husky. "I called the Register of Deeds. They can't issue a marriage license unless both parties come in. 'No exceptions,' she said. 'That is the law.' They close in twenty minutes."

She gaped up at him, goggled-eyed.

"I finagled permission from Dr. Sellers, but you'd better hurry and get our coats because I can't stand up long. Where are you parked?"

She uncurled her legs, paused a split second, then sprang into action. She bolted past him and into his room. "South side entrance," she called and emerged sporting both of their coats and the most momentous smile he had ever seen.

####

The groom wore white. His terry-cloth robe was as elegant to the bride as the finest tuxedo. She was dressed in pale pink, her corsage was of white roses, hastily ordered by Pax after telephoned instructions from his mother.

The church was not exactly crowded: only the wedding party was invited. Five people stood reverently at the altar of the hospital chapel: the pastor,

Storm as best man, Gram as a beaming matron of honor and the bride and groom.

Pax had discarded the walker to use an exquisite carved cane, a wedding gift from Storm.

After signing the marriage license, Freddie drove her husband to their apartment. He put his hand on her shoulder and allowed her to assist him up the three steps: a big man, towering above her, but leaning on her, depending on her strength, and he felt invincible.

He had not been home since the accident. He glanced around the room. The place was immaculate. He recognized his mother's handiwork. There were several bouquets of flowers, each with florist envelopes. So friends were aware of their wedding.

There was evidence also of Fred. A picture of GG and a silver framed snapshot of her friends in Arizona smiled at him from the beside night stand. His heart raced when he saw her fluffy pink bedroom slippers tucked under the bed, as tiny, it seemed to him, as doll shoes. He saw her worn brown suitcase – the one he had carried from the bus station – and above it, draped across the foot of the bed like a foreign intruder in his masculine room, was a dainty silk negligee. He suddenly knew it was not his room any more, but theirs. Tonight was the prelude of a new song for them – the weaving together of two lives. His joy knew no bounds.

He sank to his chair and scooped her into his arms. "The only things I ever wanted were you and my gallery, and I nearly lost both. Now you're Mrs. Paxton Palmer, and I'll love you forever!"

She raised her lips to his. "All I want is you." She slipped her arms around his neck. "My husband, my lover." Her whisper was a caress.

####

She propped herself up on her right elbow and studied him in the pre-dawn light. She wanted to trace the hair that followed the contour of his chest with her finger but he had refused to take a pain pill last night, and she didn't want to wake him. His sleep had been sporadic.

She watched the rising and falling of his chest with each intake of air, and love seeped through every cell in her body. How could a woman love a man more? She had quit asking herself how she had ever left him and traveled across the country with plans to marry another. They did not speak of Phoenix anymore, except in terms of Jill and Emily.

Someday, when they built their house on top of the mountain and the bedrooms were full of little boys and girls, she would tell their children about her heritage: a grandmother whose love was unceasing, and a faithful man who knew how to forgive. She would spend the rest of her life thanking the Good Lord for Pax.

The rhythm of his breathing altered. He opened his eyes and lay watching her, quizzically, his eyebrows arched with curiosity. She knew he was speculating about her thoughts.

"Are you sorry the wedding was so small?"

"Never. You and Gram were there! But I was trying not to disturb your sleep."

"Sleep? Why would I want to sleep? Darling, I am on my honeymoon!" He reached for her.

High Country Publishers, Ltd

invites you to our website to learn more about Lila Hopkins and her work. See color images of the artwork included as illustrations in this book. Read exerpts and reviews from other books by Lila Hopkins as well as other authors. Learn what's new at High Country Publishers. Link to other authors' sites, preview up-coming titles, and find out how you can order books at a discount for your group or organization.

www.highcountrypublishers.com

High Country Publishers, Ltd

Boone, NC
2002